T
FO

BY
LUCY GORDON

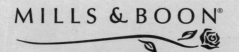

MILLS & BOON®

All the characters in this book have no existence outside the imagination of the author, and have no relation whatsoever to anyone bearing the same name or names. They are not even distantly inspired by any individual known or unknown to the author, and all the incidents are pure invention.

All Rights Reserved including the right of reproduction in whole or in part in any form. This edition is published by arrangement with Harlequin Enterprises II B.V. The text of this publication or any part thereof may not be reproduced or transmitted in any form or by any means, electronic or mechanical, including photocopying, recording, storage in an information retrieval system, or otherwise, without the written permission of the publisher.

This book is sold subject to the condition that it shall not, by way of trade or otherwise, be lent, resold, hired out or otherwise circulated without the prior consent of the publisher in any form of binding or cover other than that in which it is published and without a similar condition including this condition being imposed on the subsequent purchaser.

MILLS & BOON and MILLS & BOON with the Rose Device are registered trademarks of the publisher.

First published in Great Britain 1999
Harlequin Mills & Boon Limited,
Eton House, 18-24 Paradise Road, Richmond, Surrey TW9 1SR

© Lucy Gordon 1999

ISBN 0 263 81783 0

Set in Times Roman 10½ on 12 pt.
02-9909-48183 C1

Printed and bound in Spain
by Litografia Rosés, S.A., Barcelona

CHAPTER ONE

'WHAT are you wearing that thing for?'

Jennifer stood back to let her brother come into her house. She was already nervous about the evening to come, and his irritation only made things worse.

'I thought you bought a new dress for tonight,' he said. 'Dark blue satin, tight, slinky, very effective.' He cast a disparaging glance at her flowing evening gown of gold organdie with its demure neckline. 'You're going to a banquet, not a puritan convention.'

'I'm sorry, Trevor,' she said in a placating voice, 'but I just couldn't wear that blue satin. It's too revealing.'

'You didn't think so when you bought it.'

'Yes, I did, but I'd let you convince me it was my duty to go to this function. Since then I've got my sense of proportion back. I wish I could call the whole thing off.'

'You can't do that,' Trevor said, alarmed. 'How often must I tell you that appearances matter? Everyone knows you're representing the firm at the London Society of Commerce Banquet, and you have to be there.'

'But I was going with David.'

'And now he's dumped you—'

'He hasn't dumped me. We just—aren't seeing each other for a while.'

'Whatever. The point is you can't stay away and you can't go on your own. It would look like weakness. You've got to let the world see that you don't care.'

'But I do care,' she said sadly.

5

Jennifer had planned to attend the banquet with David Conner, the man she loved and had expected to marry. But he hadn't called her since their quarrel two weeks ago, and her heart was breaking. Her ideal evening would have been spent at home having a cup of cocoa and maybe even a good cry. Instead she was dressed up, ready to go out with a stranger.

'I hate all this business of putting on the proper mask,' she said. 'I always have.'

'Never let the enemy see you weakening,' Trevor said, reciting his favourite rule.

'And I hate having to think of everyone as the enemy.'

'It's how business is done. Come on, you've coped wonderfully well so far.'

'But you're not quite sure of me, are you? That's why you called in on your way home from work to make sure I hadn't got cold feet. Well, I have.'

Brother and sister were both part of Nortons Distribution, a trucking empire started by their grandfather, Barney Norton. They owned shares in the firm, and ran it between them since illness had forced Barney to retire. The difference was that Trevor lived and breathed business, while Jennifer had only gone into Nortons to please Barney.

Trevor was a thickset man in his thirties, no more than medium height, with a burly build. He might have been attractive if he hadn't frowned so much. Jennifer respected her brother for his dedicated work, but it was hard to like a man so short-tempered and critical.

'Be sensible,' he said now. 'Go and change into your glad rags.'

'I'm sorry, Trevor, but these rags are as glad as I'm going to get.'

He tore his hair. 'For Pete's sake! Tonight's a chance

to do some networking, make connections. Smile into their eyes, dance close. You've got the looks.'

It was true that nature had gifted Jennifer with the vivid beauty to play the role he'd outlined. Her large dark eyes dominated her oval face, and her mouth was deliciously curved in a way that could be more seductive than she was aware.

But nature had also missed something out. She completely lacked the ruthless drive and competitiveness that could have made her use her sexuality in the way Trevor expected. But he seemed not to understand this.

'You've got assets,' he said now. 'Flaunt them.'

Goaded, she said, 'Why don't you flaunt yours if it's so important to you?'

'Because mine aren't the kind that look good in skin-tight satin. The boardroom's my sphere, not the ball-room.'

'I must have been crazy to let you talk me into going to this do without David. And hiring an *escort*—even from a reputable agency. Think of it! Paying a man to accompany me!'

'I've told you: it's not like that,' he said impatiently. 'Jack's a good customer, and his grandson is an actor. A failed one, apparently, so he fills in with escort work. You did tell the agency it had to be Mike Harker, didn't you?'

'I asked for Mike Harker and nobody else. And before you ask, yes, I was careful not to let on that I've met his grandfather. As far as he knows it's an ordinary booking, so his pride won't be offended.'

'Good. Apparently he's touchy about favours, and it would have been awkward if he'd refused. What reason did you give for asking for him?'

'I said someone had told me he was very good-looking, and that was what I needed.'

'Fine. And you're quite safe. Jack assures me that Harker knows how to keep his hands to himself. Good grief! What's that?'

Jennifer followed his pointing finger. 'It's a cat,' she said, a tad defensively.

'Another of your waifs and strays, I presume?'

'I found Paws outside my back door, if that's what you mean.'

'Paws? You actually call it Paws?'

'She's a she, not an it, and her paws were the first thing I noticed. They're white and the rest of her's black.'

'Funny how every four-legged tramp seems to find its way here,' Trevor observed grimly. 'I should think the word's gone around the stray community. Drop in on Jennifer Norton. She's a soft touch.'

'Better that than a hard one,' she said quickly.

'As long as you don't bring that thing to the office, like you tried to with your last acquisition. We were just about to sign Bill Mercer up to a really profitable deal, and a damned snake slid out of your desk and nearly gave him heart failure.'

'It was a small grass snake, very sweet and perfectly harmless.'

'And then there was the gerbil—no, don't get me started on the gerbil. Anyway, it's not businesslike.'

'Well, I never was very businesslike, was I? Not the way you are, the way Barney wanted me to be. I shouldn't really be part of Nortons at all, you know. I'm not cut out for the cut and thrust. Sometimes I think I should get out while I'm still in my twenties, and try something else.'

'You can't do that to Barney,' Trevor said, aghast. 'After all he's done for us! I agree, you're a fish out of water, but you've always been his pet, and if you defect it will break his heart.'

'I know,' she said with a helpless sigh, for this was the argument she'd used to herself a hundred times. She couldn't hurt Barney, and the knowledge was like fetters.

'If you'd just use your head a little more,' Trevor said now. 'Stop making decisions that you haven't thought through. You're far too impulsive.'

It was true. Jennifer was warm-hearted and spontaneous, and these qualities often conflicted with the demands of her work. She had brains, and she'd learned the business thoroughly, but people and animals would always matter to her more.

She didn't try to explain this to Trevor. She'd failed too often in the past. She merely contented herself with saying, 'Tonight you're the one who hasn't thought it through. The whole idea is mad.'

'Nonsense! Look, I've got to go. Chin up!'

He gave her cheek a peck and departed.

Left alone, Jennifer sighed. When they were younger she and Trevor had been close, but now that seemed a long time ago. When she tried to argue with him she was out of her depth. In fact, she increasingly felt that her life had been taken over by forces outside her control, and never more so than tonight.

Trevor had spoken of what Barney had done for them, and it was true that he'd taken them in when their mother had died, when she'd been twelve and Trevor sixteen. Nobody had known where their father was, since he'd abandoned his family some two years earlier. There'd been a divorce and he'd moved abroad with his new lover. There had only been their grandfather.

Barney was affectionate, but his idea of childcare had been to scoop them up into his hectic life, taking them with him from place to place. It had been interesting and fun, but there had been nothing to make Jennifer feel less of an orphan.

Barney couldn't replace the father who'd deserted her, but she'd loved him, and striven to please him. She'd worked hard at school, enjoying his praise when she got top marks, and gradually coming to accept that she would go into the business.

'I'm really looking forward to having you two as my partners,' he'd say happily.

Trevor had joined Nortons as soon as he'd left school, and Barney had started preparing for the day his beloved Jennifer would follow. She hadn't had the heart to tell him that she would rather work with animals. To disappoint him would have been to risk losing his love, and she'd long ago learned how painful that could be.

So she'd entered the firm and performed every task well, making him proud of her. When his health had failed, five years ago, Trevor and Jennifer had been ready to take over the reins, leaving him to a happy retirement. To all outward appearances she was a glamorous, successful businesswoman, but inside she felt trapped, and a failure.

Now here she was, ready to attend a function that didn't interest her in the company of a man she didn't know, more imprisoned than ever by the expectations of others. And wishing with all her heart there was some way of escape.

Steven Leary stopped outside the apartment door and looked at his shabby surroundings in dismay. Once his friend Mike Harker had been a wit, with matinée idol looks, destined for stage and film stardom. But that had been twelve years ago. Steven had kept in touch, but they hadn't met for five years. Mike's career had flopped, and he now lived in this dump.

The door opened a crack, revealing one bloodshot eye. 'Who are you?' came a muffled voice.

'Mike? It's me—Steven.'

'Hell. Steven?' Mike drew him inside and quickly shut the door. 'I was afraid you were the landlord.'

They exclaimed over each other, and studied the difference that the years had made. Mike was still handsome, although bleary eyes and a red nose spoiled the effect.

'Stay clear,' he said, waving Steven back. 'I'm a walking flu germ.'

'Did I pick a bad time?' Steven asked, indicating Mike's white tie and tails on a coat hanger. 'You look as if you're going to a première.'

Mike gave him a wry look. 'If I was into premières, would I be living here?'

Over coffee they exchanged awkward conversation. Steven felt embarrassed to ask Are you still an actor?, and even more embarrassed to talk about his own success.

'I remember when you joined Charteris Enterprises,' Mike said. 'I said you'd end up running the place, and you did.'

'It's no big deal,' Steven said, speaking less than the truth. Charteris was a huge, powerful conglomerate, and its achievements were his pride and joy.

'You ought to be in bed,' he told Mike.

'I have to go out. I survive by working for an escort agency, and I've got a job tonight.'

'You're a gigolo?' Steven exclaimed, aghast.

'No, dammit, I'm not a gigolo! It's perfectly respectable. If a woman has to go to some function and she hasn't got an escort, she calls my agency and hires me. I just have to be attentive and make the right impression. She goes home to her bed and I go home to mine.'

'Which is where you should be right now. You can't escort a woman in this state. You'll give her flu.'

'And she'll give me money, so that I can stop avoiding the landlord.'

'Tell your agency to send someone else.'

'Too late.' Mike went off into a coughing fit.

'What's she like?'

'Dunno. Never met her. Her name's Jennifer Norton, and that's all I know. It's a commercial function, so she's probably a hard-faced business-type—mid-forties, too busy making money to have a real relationship, so she calls Rent-A-Man.'

'Get to bed,' Steven said firmly. 'I'll go in your place.'

'But they said she asked for me specially.'

'I thought you didn't know her?'

'I don't. But apparently someone recommended me.'

'Could she have seen you on television?'

'No such luck!'

'So she doesn't know what you look like?'

'No way. But she wanted a real looker.'

Steven grinned, not in the least offended. 'And I'm Frankenstein's monster?'

'Cut it out! You always had more than your share of girls, I remember. Can't think why, when you treated them so badly.'

'I never laid myself out to please them, if that's what you mean. Couldn't see the point. My dad used to say women were like buses. There'd always be another one along soon.' He gave a crack of laughter. 'Mind you, he got well clear of Mum before he said it.'

It was true that Steven didn't have the perfect, regular features that distinguished Mike, but many women found him vitally attractive. He was tall, dark, and powerfully made, with broad shoulders, and the set of his head gave him an air of natural authority. His lean face could scowl or laugh with equal fervour. Thick brows shadowed brown eyes radiating a fierce energy that gave his face its striking character. His mouth was wide and generous. It could form a grin that was predatory, even wolfish, but his smiles were delightful. When in a light-hearted mood he could be charming.

A man who stood out in a crowd. A man that another man, or a woman, would think twice before crossing. Perhaps a man to be feared. But not a man that a woman would choose as a gallant escort.

'You can't go and that's final,' he said. 'I'll use your name, and I'll be on my best behaviour. I'd better dash home for my evening rig.'

'No time. She's expecting me in twenty minutes. You'll have to wear mine. Luckily we're about the same size.' Mike coughed again. 'I hope you haven't caught my flu.'

'I never catch anything,' Steven said. 'I'm invulnerable. What are you looking at out of the window?'

'That shiny monster, with this year's registration, parked under my window. If it's yours you'll never pass as a penniless actor.'

'Thanks for the tip. I'll park a few streets away from her house and walk. Now get to bed.'

Her escort was late, which was fine by Jennifer. It gave her time to feed Paws and let her out one last time.

'Hurry up,' she said. 'He'll be here soon—if I'm unlucky.'

Paws reappeared two minutes later, wet from a puddle, and promptly demonstrated her loyalty by leaping into her new mistress's lap.

'Oh, no!' Jennifer wailed, surveying the marks over her dress. 'I can't believe you did that!'

She made a dash for the bedroom, tore off the muddy garment, and began rummaging through her other evening wear, desperately hoping that her worst fears weren't going to be realised.

But they were. Of two other possible gowns, one was at the cleaner's and one had a small tear. Bit by bit her options narrowed down until there was only the dark blue satin left.

'You ungrateful animal!' she chided Paws. 'I took you in, and now look what you've done to me. Oh, well, I suppose there's no help for it.'

Reluctantly she drew on the dress, which was even more daring than she'd realised when she'd bought it. To her horror, the lines of her underwear showed. There was only one thing to do, and that was remove every stitch underneath.

When she'd finished she had the perfect, smooth lines that the dress demanded. Its tight contours flattered her tiny waist and flat stomach, but the neckline was scandalously low. She possessed the generous bosom to carry it off, but still, it was going to take nerve. And her nerve was fast slipping away.

Her rich, dark brown hair was swept up in an elegantly ornate style. To go with the dress she donned a necklace and earrings made of glittering diamonds. Now she looked like a sophisticated young woman who could cope with anything life threw at her. She only wished she felt like one.

She finished just in time. The doorbell was shrilling. She put her head up, took a deep breath, and went to answer. And as soon as she opened her front door she knew that she'd made the mistake of her life.

The man's looks were striking, if not classically handsome. He radiated an air of arrogance and fierce will. In the very first moment, as they stood looking at each other, Jennifer realised that he was appraising her, his eyes taking a leisurely tour of her form.

She began to be self-conscious about the revealing dress. His gaze made her feel naked, and he was clearly enjoying every inch of her, which made her indignant. After all, he was her employee. Worse still, she saw an ironic gleam in his eyes, as though he understood her thoughts and was amused by them.

In short, she'd expected a tailor's dummy and gotten a man instead.

Embarrassment flooded her. It hadn't occurred to her that she was exposing herself as a woman who had to pay for an escort. But he saw the truth. She found her voice. 'Good evening, Mr Harker. You're a little late, but no matter.'

'My apologies,' he said, in a voice that didn't sound apologetic. 'I had an emergency to deal with, but now I'm all yours.' He spread his hands in a gesture that took in his own appearance. 'All present and correct,' he announced. 'Fingernails specially scrubbed for the occasion.' He offered them to her view, but still with the teasing air that unsettled her.

'Oh, my goodness!' she exclaimed suddenly. 'Those cufflinks.'

She guessed that his 'dress' cufflinks were all a failed

actor could afford, but they looked cheap and nasty, as if he'd bought them off a market stall.

'They're my best,' the man said brusquely. 'What's wrong with them?'

'Nothing, I—' Jennifer struggled to find a polite way of saying what she meant. It was hard. 'They're not quite—I mean, they don't really go with—perhaps I could suggest—just a moment.'

She hurried to her room and found the cufflinks she'd bought for David's upcoming birthday. They were silver, studded with tiny diamonds, and they'd cost her a fortune. She suppressed the little pang they gave her and closed her fingers tightly over them.

Her escort's strongly marked eyebrows rose in surprise when she asked him to hold out his hands. She removed the cheap items and fitted the luxurious cufflinks in their place. Glancing up, she found his eyes on her, and their cool mockery sent a wave of heat flooding through her body.

He regarded the diamonds on his cuffs, and his eyes gleamed as they appraised the diamonds about her neck and on her ears. 'I'm glad I go with your jewellery,' he murmured.

She refused to respond to his mockery. 'Here are the keys to my car, Mr Harker. Shall we go?'

As she opened the garage door on her sleek, four-wheeled beauty, she began to have qualms. 'Perhaps I'd better drive,' she said. She held out her hand for the keys, but Steven didn't move.

'Get in the car,' he said, with a quiet firmness that astonished her. 'I'm here to escort you, and I'll do the job properly. It wouldn't look good for you to be driving. People might guess that you've had to hire me.'

She bit back a retort and got into the passenger seat.

He began backing the car out as expertly as if he did it
every day. She wondered where he'd learned that deft
handling of a powerful vehicle. It had taken her a week
before she was as skilled.

'Which way?' he asked.

'Central London. Go to Trafalgar Square and I'll direct you from there.'

When they were on the road he said casually, 'So,
what story do we tell people?'

'Story?'

'About us. If someone asks, we have to say the same
thing. When did we meet?'

'Oh—last week.'

'That's a bit recent. Why not last month?'

'No,' she said quickly. 'Not as long ago as that.'

'I see. You were going out with someone else then?
Why aren't you with him tonight?'

'Because we—we had a disagreement.'

'Who dumped who?'

'We separated by mutual consent,' she said stiffly.

'You mean he walked out on you?'

'I mean no such thing.'

'Will he be there tonight?'

'Possibly.'

'Then you'd better tell me his name, just in case.'

'His name is David Conner,' she said stiffly.

'Have you worked out how we met?'

'No—I don't know—I'll think of something,' she said
distractedly. She was growing more unhappy by the minute.

'I'm surprised to find you so disorganised. We're
nearly at Trafalgar Square. Direct me.'

She complied, adding, 'We're going to Catesby House
for the London Society of Commerce Banquet. *Careful!*'

'Sorry! My hand slipped on the wheel,' Steven said hastily. In fact, he'd had a nasty shock. There would be people there who knew him. He made a rapid decision.

'You'd better know,' he said, 'my real name isn't Mike Harker.'

'You mean it's a stage name?'

'No, I— Never mind. My name is Steven Leary. We're nearly there. Quickly, tell me something about yourself.'

'My name is Jennifer Norton. I'm the granddaughter of Barney Norton of Nortons Distribution—'

'Nortons Distribution?' Steven echoed. 'Trucks and depots?'

'Yes,' she said, surprised to find him so knowledge-able. 'Our organisation is the best of its kind in the country, and we're rapidly expanding in Europe.' She suddenly remembered who he was. 'Never mind that.'

'Yes, don't say anything too complex,' he said affably. 'My one braincell might not be able to cope.'

She refused to let him needle her. 'Take this next turning and you'll find a car park.'

As he switched off the engine Jennifer went to open her door. 'Wait,' Steven ordered calmly. He walked around the car and opened the door for her, holding out his hand to assist her. 'After all, this is what I'm here for,' he said, with a grin.

'Thank you,' she said, placing her hand in his.

She half missed her footing as she stepped out, but his fingers tightened, holding her steady, and she had an unnerving sense of vibrant power streaming through him and communicating itself through the contact of their skin. For a moment her heart beat faster.

She turned to reach back into the car for her velvet stole, but he was there before her, whisking it out and settling it around her bare shoulders. She couldn't suppress the tremor that went through her at his touch, and involuntarily she glanced up to meet his eyes. She found them fixed on her with a look that brought the colour flooding into her cheeks.

'You're beautiful,' he said seriously. 'In fact, you're sensational. I'll be a proud man, with you on my arm. No, don't say it!' He held up a finger to silence her, although she was too taken aback to speak. 'You don't care whether I'm proud of you or not. It's not part of our bargain. Well, I don't care whether *you* care or not. I'm telling you, you're a knock-out!'

Something was making it hard for her to speak. 'Thank you,' she stammered at last. 'It's nice to know that my escort approves of me.'

'I don't approve of you,' Steven said wryly. 'I disapprove of this whole situation. A woman who looks like you shouldn't have to hire a man, and if she does there's something badly wrong in her life. But you're gorgeous, sexy, and an incitement to every man to do something he'll regret. I only wish I had time to explore that contradiction.'

'My contradictions don't concern you,' she said, her cheeks flaming.

'They would if I decided to let them,' he said carelessly. 'What a pity that I don't have time!' He drew one finger slowly down her cheek. 'We should be going inside.'

'Yes,' she said, remembering, with an effort, why they were there. 'We should.'

Jennifer had attended many functions at Catesby House, and was familiar with its plush red and gilt interior, sweeping stairway and glittering chandeliers. But tonight she seemed to be seeing everything for the first time. The lights were more dazzling, the colours of the other women's dresses more vivid, and the black and white of the men more intense than she remembered ever noticing before.

She went to the cloakroom to deposit her stole. As she emerged to where Steven was waiting for her at the foot of the staircase she had the chance to observe him from a distance, against other men.

The comparison was all in his favour. He was almost the tallest man there. Certainly his shoulders were the broadest, his air the most impressive. But what struck her most was the confidence and authority that radiated from him. He looked like a predator, appraising lesser beings prior to devouring them. She'd seen that aura before, in men who headed great corporations. How did an unemployed actor come to have it?

Actor. Of course. He'd assumed the right role. Anxious to have a good atmosphere between them, she approached him with a smile. 'Congratulations,' she said warmly.

'I beg your pardon?'

'You've got right into the part. You look as if you belong here.'

'Thank you,' he said with suspicious meekness. 'I'm rather nervous among all these important people.'

'They're not really important. They only fancy they are because they've got money. Most business folk don't matter half as much as they think they do.' With a flash of mischief, she added, 'Just look down your nose at them, and they'll take you for one of themselves. I'm expecting you to be a big success.'

His lips twitched. 'You don't feel you got cheated on the deal, then?'

'On the contrary, I think I might have a bargain.'

'Maybe I didn't do so badly myself.' He offered her his arm. 'Shall we go?'

Together they climbed the broad stairs and entered the huge ballroom that was already crowded. Steven's sharp eyes saw at once that Jennifer outshone every other woman in the room. She knew how to choose perfume too. The elusive aroma that reached him was warm, with the faintest hint of musk. It wasn't the perfume of a young girl, but a woman, with all that implied.

He wondered what kind of lover had touched her heart. Had she chosen a giant among men? And what was she like when she was with him? Did her curved mouth grow tender and her dark eyes glow with desire?

They moved through the crowd, smiling and uttering greetings. Several people knew him, and Steven had a nervous time steering her away from them. He would be lucky to get through tonight without discovery, he realised.

'Come to the bar,' he muttered. 'There's something we need to talk about while I get you a drink.'

'I'll have an orange juice, since I'll be driving home.'

'Two orange juices,' Steven told the barman. He grinned at Jennifer. 'Just in case you change your mind.'

'Meaning you think you can change it for me?' she challenged him.

'Is that what I meant? Thanks for letting me know.'

His eyes were teasing, and Jennifer couldn't help smiling back. 'That's exactly what you meant,' she said. She turned back to look at the room. And then the smile froze on her face.

David was standing a few feet away from her.

CHAPTER TWO

JENNIFER had wondered if David would be here. Now she realized that she'd always secretly expected him. Her heart skipped a beat at the sight of his perfect features under thick, wavy, fair hair.

He looked in her direction and Jennifer saw the shock in his eyes. In another moment he would hold out his hands to her and all their differences would be forgotten. But he stayed frozen, his mouth opening and closing. He seemed confused. Then a young woman laid a hand on his arm, and he bowed his handsome head attentively towards her.

Jennifer stood there, stunned. David had turned away from her. There was a bleak, blind look in her eyes, and she forgot everything else, including Steven, watching her face closely.

Perhaps, she thought, David too had hired a companion. But a glance at the young woman banished that thought. She was mousy, and didn't know how to make the best of herself. This wasn't a professional. She was 'real'.

Jennifer's insides twisted at the thought that David had found someone else so soon. Then the girl smiled at him. It was a gentle, heartfelt smile, and it made her face charming. Jennifer was unable to control her little gasp. Steven heard it, and his eyes narrowed with interest.

'So that's him,' he murmured in Jennifer's ear.

'Him—who?'

'The pretty boy with the dull girl.'

'I don't know what you mean by pretty boy—'

'He's like a sugar figure on top of a wedding cake.'

'Can we drop this?' she asked with an effort.

'But why? I'm only here to show him that you don't give a damn. So let's show him—unless you're scared?'

'Of course not,' she said quickly.

'Then take the bull by the horns.'

'You're right.' She advanced on David with her hands outstretched. 'David! How lovely to see you.'

He too recovered himself, and she knew he hadn't expected to find her here with another man. 'Jennifer,' he said. 'What a—a lovely surprise.'

'But you knew I planned to come.'

'Yes—er—yes, of course. It's just that—let me introduce you to Penny.' He hastily drew forward the young woman, who gave Jennifer a nervous look, followed immediately by her delightful smile.

'This is Steven Leary,' Jennifer said. As the men shook hands she began to feel more confident. At least David knew she wasn't sitting forlornly at home, waiting for the phone to ring, and he need never know how often she'd done just that.

She slipped her arm through Steven's and he responded on cue, smiling into her eyes with a theatrical intensity that was almost fatuous. She had a mad desire to giggle, as though the two of them were engaged in a private joke that nobody else understood. Not even David.

He was frowning uneasily, as though the sight of her with another man displeased him. But then Penny claimed his attention and he turned away. Jennifer kept her head up and her smile in place, but it was hard.

Fifty round tables filled the room, each seating eight

guests. Jennifer didn't know whether to be glad or dismayed to find that she was at the same table as David and Penny. They were almost opposite her, so she could see how gallantly he drew out her chair. He was always an attentive dinner companion, Jennifer thought wistfully. It made him charming to be with. She averted her eyes.

'Tell me about David Conner,' Steven said. 'What does he do?'

'He owns a small firm making machine tools,' Jennifer said.

'Did he start it himself?'

'No, his father left it to him.'

The meal kept them occupied for a while. Steven played his part to perfection, attending to all her wants and smiling. Then there were speeches. Jennifer was facing the top table, but David and Penny had to turn around, so she could watch them without being seen. She noticed that David didn't rest his hand on his companion's arm, but sometimes he would lean close to speak to her, so that their hair touched.

The speeches ended and the mood became relaxed. People began drifting from table to table. One or two dropped by to talk to her. She did some useful networking, and when she'd finished she noticed that Steven was sitting with David and Penny. David was talking earnestly, and Steven was listening with a frown of concentration that made Jennifer wonder if he were concealing boredom.

'How about asking me to dance?' she said.

'My lady has only to command,' Steven replied, and led her onto the floor for a waltz.

'You don't know what a rare pleasure it is to dance

with a woman tall enough to look me in the eye,' he observed. 'Usually I get a crick in my neck.'

'I thought I ought to rescue you from David.'

'Afraid all his serious talk would be above my head, huh?'

'What did you tell him about us?'

'That I was your toyboy, of course.'

'Can't you be serious for a minute?'

'I'll tell you this seriously. I'm not sure I ought to help you get him back. You might end up married to him, and how would I ever forgive myself?'

'What do you mean?'

'He's not the man you need. You'd always be fighting with him for the mirror.'

'What nonsense!'

'It isn't nonsense, Jenny—'

'Don't,' she said quickly. 'Only David calls me Jenny.'

'It's the wrong name for you anyway. Jenny is a little brown wren, and you're a bird of paradise.'

'Don't be so sure,' she said lightly. 'I might turn out to be a cawing rook instead.'

He broke into laughter. It was a rich, pleasant sound, and several people glanced at them, including David. Immediately she turned up the wattage on her smile, focusing on Steven's face.

'OK,' he said, understanding at once. 'If that's how you want to play it—' He tightened his arm in the small of her back, drawing her against him, and an ardent look came into his eyes. 'You're gorgeous. I hope David appreciates you.'

'Of course he does.'

'Has he mentioned marriage?'

She hesitated. 'In his own way.'

'What does that mean?'

'In actions,' she said reluctantly, 'not words.'

'Don't fool yourself, Jennifer. That "actions not words" argument is how women convince themselves that a man has said something when he hasn't. You want him to propose and he won't. Is that why you quarrelled?'

'Never mind.'

'Of course I mind. Until midnight I'm your new lover, madly jealous of the man you're in love with. You *are* in love with him, aren't you?'

'Completely.'

'More fool you! What *was* the quarrel about?'

How could she stop this man? He seemed to have an hypnotic power that made it natural to tell him whatever he wanted to know.

But it was hard to analyse the quarrel because she wasn't sure what it had been about. They'd been discussing a problem David had had with his firm. To her the solution had been obvious, and she'd been happy to help him. Suddenly she'd looked up to see him watching her strangely.

'You know more about this than I do, don't you?' he'd asked quietly.

Even then she hadn't seen the danger, but had answered cheerfully. 'It's being with that old rascal, my grandfather. Some of it rubs off. Look, darling, all you have to do is—'

But he'd stopped her there, accusing her of trying to take charge. She'd denied it indignantly, and things had escalated. By the time they parted they'd covered so much ground that the original disagreement had become lost.

'It had nothing to do with marriage,' she said now, at last.

'I'm glad. You're worth a better man than David Conner.'

'Don't say that!' she protested quickly.

'Well done! I like you with that glowing light in your eyes. Don't keep trying to watch him. You'll spoil your effect. Concentrate on me. I think you're a knock-out, plus you've got courage and spirit.'

'Do you always talk to your clients like this?'

'My—? Well, it's true that I don't do this often,' Steven said, recovering quickly from his slip. 'I tend to tell people the blunt truth instead of murmuring sweet nothings. Smile at me. He's looking.'

Jennifer offered up her most dazzling smile and he returned it, gazing deep into her eyes. 'That's fine,' he murmured. 'Mind you, you're more impressive when you're annoyed.'

'If you dare to tell me I look beautiful when I'm angry I'll—I'll step on your toe.'

'I promise not to say anything so corny.'

'Good.'

'Even though it's true.'

She saw his lips twitch and couldn't stop herself from responding. The next moment she was joining in his laughter. 'Oh, go to the devil!' she said lightly.

'Certainly. With you in my arms I'll waltz to the mouth of hell and back.' His eyes flickered in David's direction, and he murmured through his smile, 'You've got him worried.'

'Who?'

'David. Don't tell me you've forgotten the poor sap?'

'Of course not,' she said, too quickly. It was true that

she'd been so intrigued by this man that David had briefly slipped from her mind.

'Let's give him something to really worry about,' Steven suggested. He drew her closer still, looking down deep into her eyes. 'I love the cut of your dress,' he whispered.

She knew he meant her low neckline, and to her dismay she started to blush. She was one of those lucky women who could blush attractively, her cheeks going a delicate pink—something the man holding her close noticed with interest.

'You're the most beautiful woman here,' he told her.

'Stop saying things like that,' Jennifer whispered.

'You're paying me to say them,' he reminded her.

She caught her breath with shock. She'd been caught up in this man's seductive spell, her senses vibrating with the power that streamed from him. And it was all a delusion. She'd bought his compliments, and they meant nothing.

'Well, since you're under my orders,' she said in a shaking voice, 'I'm telling you to stop.'

'You hired me to make David Conner jealous, and that's what I'm going to do.'

'I hired you as an accessory, to be useful to my firm,' she said quickly, remembering what Trevor had said.

'Nonsense, that's just the "party line". It's David you care about. Though just why is a mystery to me.'

He raised her chin with his fingers. She couldn't resist him. Suddenly her heart was beating madly. She tried to ignore her own sensations and remember only that she was playing a part. But she could hardly remember the part, or why she was playing it. It was like floating in a dream.

This arrogantly assured man had the nerve to brush

his fingertips over her lips. Jennifer drew a shuddering breath, astounded by the feelings coursing through her. This must stop. She must *make* him stop. But she did nothing. Nor could she speak.

She felt his touch drift across her mouth, along the line of her jaw and down her neck. Then his hand was cupping her head, drawing it closer as he lowered his lips to hers. Jennifer had a devastating sense of losing control. Everything about this evening had been a shock, and most shocking of all was the pleasure that possessed her as soon as his mouth rested on hers.

She lost all sense of time and space. She could no longer hear the band, or see the other couples circling around them. She was moving through the heavens in a dance that would last until the end of eternity. Her heart was beating wildly and she could hardly breathe.

'You must let me go,' she whispered.

'If I had my way I'd never let you go,' he growled. 'I'd whisk you out of here to some place where they couldn't find us, and discover what kind of a woman you really are. The answer might come as a surprise to you too.'

'How dare you?'

'Strange, isn't it? But I already know you as David Conner never will. I know what I want from you, which I'll bet is a damned sight more than he does.'

To her dismay the words 'I know what I want from you' sent a thrill through her. There had been a steely resolution in his tone that she'd never heard before from any man. She loved David for his gentleness and sweet temperament, but in a corner of her heart she had to admit he lacked decisiveness.

Not that decisiveness was all-important. She'd always

told herself that. But in the arms of this purposeful man she felt a unique quiver of response that alarmed her.

She heard him mutter a soft 'Damn!' and came out of her dream to realise that the music was ending. The dancers were slowing and she was in Steven Leary's arms, seeing the shock in his eyes, knowing that it mirrored the shock in her own. And nothing would ever be the same again.

For the next hour Jennifer functioned on automatic. Her mind was still whirling from the devastating encounter with Steven, and her flesh too seemed to be in turmoil, tingling with the memory of his touch.

Out of the corner of her eye she saw him waltzing with Penny. At last he appeared at her side again, taking her hand and leading her to the bar, where he procured her an orange juice. 'You must be ready for some refreshment,' he said. 'So am I. I've been working for you.'

'I saw you dancing with Penny,' she said, taking his meaning. 'How did you find her?'

'She moves too correctly. I prefer a woman who dances with a man as though she wants to make love with him.' His eyes challenged her.

'I can imagine,' Jennifer said, speaking awkwardly to conceal the fact that waves of heat were chasing themselves through her. 'Is that the only fault you can find with poor Penny?'

'She says "Yes" and "No" and keeps missing the step because she's trying to keep her eyes on David. She's his secretary, by the way, and he only invited her this afternoon.' He heard her quick sigh of relief and said mischievously, 'It looks as if he left it until the last minute, hoping you'd call. He doesn't understand you because he's full of himself. He's happier with a girl who isn't as pretty as he is. You two were bound to break up.'

'David and I haven't broken up—not finally.'

'You have if Penny has anything to do with it. She's keen on him.'

With a flash of spirit she said, 'I can take him back any time I want.'

'But is he worth taking?'

'Yes,' she said defiantly.

'All right. Come on.' Steven led her over to where David and Penny were talking. Charmingly he drew Penny away, leaving David and Jennifer together. David drew a deep breath.

'How have you been keeping?' he asked politely.

I've been yearning for you to phone, and breaking my heart when you didn't, she thought. *I've cried when nobody was looking, and tried to understand what I did wrong.*

'Well, you know what it's like at this time of year,' she said with a laugh. 'The work just keeps crowding in and I haven't had a moment to myself. I expect it's the same with you.'

Let me see the old look in your eyes.

'Well, yes, I've been pretty busy,' he agreed. 'In fact, I've been away for most of the last two weeks. That's why I wasn't there if you called me.'

'No,' she said tensely, 'actually, I didn't.'

'Of course not. I didn't mean— Well, anyway…'

He finished with a helpless shrug and a smile. Jennifer caught her breath at that smile, which illuminated his boyishly handsome face.

'David,' she said impulsively, stretching out her hand to him. In another moment he would say her name, and their estrangement would be over.

'Don't stand about talking, darling!' Steven appeared out of nowhere and seized hold of her. 'The night is young. Let's dance!'

Before Jennifer could protest she was swept willy-nilly onto the floor, held firmly in Steven's arms.

'Why did you do that?' she protested. 'He was just going to— What do you think you're doing?'

'Saving you from making a terrible mistake. I was watching, and he wasn't "just going to". You were just going to fall at his feet.'

'That's none of your—! I wouldn't have done any such thing.'

'Your face said differently. Is that all it takes? He gives that little boy smile, and a sensible woman goes ga-ga?'

'Let me go at once. You're right out of order.'

She tried to struggle free but he drew her closer, holding her tight so that his lips were close to her ear, and his body moved against her. 'You should be thanking me, you ungrateful woman! If you'd caved in at the first test your relationship would never have recovered.'

'What do you mean, "test"?'

'It was your first meeting since the quarrel, and you were the one who blinked. I'll bet he was talking about himself. Not about you, or the two of you, but himself. He looks the kind of self-centred idiot who thinks all roads lead back to him.'

She would have died rather than admit he was right. Her heart ached with disappointment that David hadn't come up to scratch, and it hurt that Steven had seen it.

'What is it with women like you that you have to fall for weak men?'

'He's not weak. He's not arrogantly macho, if that's

what you mean. Some men don't feel the need to be. It's a question of confidence.'

'And what did you do to damage his confidence?'

Jennifer drew a sharp breath. 'That's a lousy thing to say!'

'Too near the truth?'

Suddenly she'd had more than she could take for one night. 'I think it's time I went home,' she said.

'Right. Put your hand through my arm and we'll make a grand exit. Head up!'

Jennifer drove the first mile in silence before asking, 'Where shall I take you?'

'Just drop me at the next bus stop.'

'I'm prepared to drive you home.'

'Thank you, but the bus stop will do.'

'There's no need to be a martyr,' Jennifer said patiently. 'Tell me where you live.'

'Must we finish up with an argument?'

'What does it matter?' she said despondently. 'This whole evening has been a disaster.'

'Not the whole evening,' he reminded her. 'There were a few enjoyable moments—'

To her dismay she could feel her cheeks burning at the reminder. To make sure he didn't suspect, she spoke stiffly. 'Forget them, Mr Leary. I've already done so.'

'That I don't believe.'

'These things happen. People get carried away. It means nothing.'

'You act like that with every man? Shame on you!'

She could hear the grin in his voice and strove to keep her dignity. 'You know what I mean. The night's over and we'll never meet again.'

'Think so?'

'Not while I can prevent it.'

'A reckless man might interpret that as a challenge.'

'Don't try.'

'I'll bet you another kiss that you contact me before the week is out.'

'We're approaching a bus stop. Goodnight, Mr Leary.'

As she pulled in to the kerb Steven began to fidget with the diamond cufflinks. 'You'd better have these back.'

She didn't want them. She could never give them to David now. Weariness and disappointment made her say, 'There's no need. Keep them to console yourself for losing your bet. You'll get a good price for them.'

Steven already had the door open, but at this he stopped and regarded her coolly. 'Perhaps I'd rather wear them to remind me of you.'

'I'd rather you didn't,' she said, wishing that he would get out and leave her alone with her sadness. 'I want to forget everything about tonight.'

'And I don't mean to let you,' he said firmly, putting a hand behind her head and drawing her hard against him. It was a swift, decisive movement that left her no time to resist. Before she could think, his mouth was on hers, devastating her with the power and sensuality of his kiss.

He kissed her with fierce purpose. His lips were firm and warm, moving over hers insistently, allowing her no time to protest, to think, or do anything except respond.

'Stop this,' she said in a hoarse whisper.

'I don't want to stop,' he growled. 'And nor do you.'

She tried to deny it, to refuse him the easy mastery that he took for granted, but her blood was pounding and she couldn't think of the words. And besides, his mouth had silenced her again.

He kissed her as though he had all the time in the

world, teasing her with swift flickerings of his tongue against her lips. Those expert movements sent electricity sparkling and crackling along her nerves until every part of her seemed to be sensitised to him.

Her mind protested, but he'd found a way past thought, direct to her deepest, most sensual instincts. He was a master of the skills of the body, a master of provocation and incitement, and if she let him he would soon become her master too.

But the hand she raised to fend him off assumed a will of its own and touched his face instead. Perhaps her fingers curved about his neck and into his hair. She wasn't sure. She was beyond being sure of anything except that she was caught up in a bittersweet delight. She was mad to have let this happen, but it was too late now.

She felt his fingers drift lower to her tiny waist, sliding over the smooth satin that covered the womanly curve of her hip.

But something stopped him. She felt him grow tense, then draw back, releasing her lips abruptly. He was breathing hard and his eyes glinted. 'You madwoman,' he growled. 'Coming out with a stranger like this! You're not wearing anything under this dress. Are you crazy to do such a thing?' He gave her a little shake.

'This shouldn't have happened,' she cried. 'If you'd— you weren't meant to—'

'The hired help was supposed to keep his hands to himself, wasn't he?' he said angrily.

'Get out of this car,' she said in a shaking voice. 'Get out at once. Do you hear?'

'Yes, perhaps I'd better escape while we're both still safe.' He got out and closed the door, still looking at her through the open window. 'Until we meet again.'

'We never will.'

'Don't be stupid,' he said harshly. 'You know better than that.'

There was only one way to silence him and she took it, slamming her foot on the accelerator pedal and driving away. A glance into her rearview mirror showed him still standing there, watching her, a scowl on his face.

CHAPTER THREE

JENNIFER was late getting to her desk next morning. She'd overslept, after spending most of the night tossing and turning. She was horrified at the way she'd succumbed to the physical attractions of a man she barely knew, but he'd triggered sensations that had alarmed her.

She'd finally dozed off, and awoken with one certainty fixed in her mind. She must never, ever see Steven Leary again. He could make her act like a stranger to herself. Or rather, he could bring her up against the fact that she had no clear idea who she was.

She was Barney Norton's beautiful, successful granddaughter, and the apple of his eye. But she was also someone who took in waifs and strays, because she felt like a waif herself, and without them her life was lonely. She was a top businesswoman who was bored with business. And somewhere deep inside she was still the little ten-year-old girl whose adored father had walked out without a backward glance.

She'd thought of David, whose gentle manners and kindly nature she loved. Neither of her menfolk had appreciated him.

'He's very sound,' Barney had said, damning him with faint praise. 'Sound', in Barney's vocabulary, meant uninspired.

Trevor had put it even more bluntly. 'He'll never set the Thames on fire.'

But she didn't want a man who would set the Thames on fire. She wanted a man whose steadiness she could

rely on, and David fitted the bill perfectly. At least he
had, until their quarrel. But that was her fault, she assured herself. She'd offended him by the clumsy way
she'd tried to help. When they made up she would be
more careful.

Safe, dependable David had never tried to rush her,
never demanded. True, there had been moments when
she'd wished he could be a little more decisive, but he
was also vulnerable in a way that touched her heart.
Jennifer's nature had a bedrock of quiet strength, and
while she needed a man to hold onto, she also needed a
man who would hold onto her. She couldn't turn away
from anyone who needed her protection, and David had
only to smile and say, 'What would I do without you?'
to make her melt.

That was her touchstone, the reason she loved David
tenderly. It was why she would never love Steven Leary,
who hadn't a hint of vulnerability in his nature.

What had happened between them was something
apart, a warning that her sensuality could betray her into
the arms of the wrong man if she wasn't careful. But
she would heed the warning. Nothing was going to come
between her and David.

She'd reached the office in such a rush that she was
only vaguely aware that her staff were giving her curious
looks. As always, her first task was to check the firm's
share price. What she discovered made her stare at the
computer screen, frowning.

'That can't be right,' she murmured. 'Why should we
go up by that much since yesterday?'

But the same figures appeared again. Next moment
her phone rang. 'You'd better get in here and let me
know what's been going on,' Trevor growled, and
hung up.

Puzzled, Jennifer crossed the corridor to his office. 'I didn't understand any of that,' she said, closing his door behind her.

'I'm talking about you and Charteris Enterprises.'

'I've had nothing to do with Charteris Enterprises.'

'Oh, no?' Trevor said sarcastically. 'And you weren't with their managing director last night, I suppose?'

'You know where I was last night—at the banquet with Mike Harker. No, wait. He said his real name was Steven Leary.'

'He *told* you that? And you didn't hear alarm bells?'

Trevor shoved a newspaper across his desk. Jennifer's eyed widened at the picture of herself and Steven dancing smoochily. The caption gave details of the banquet, of herself, and of *'Steven Leary, Managing Director of Charteris Enterprises, who is also a major stock-holder and chief architect of its success.'*

'Now people think we're doing a deal with Charteris, and that's why our shares have soared,' Trevor told her.

'I don't understand this,' Jennifer said distractedly. 'You told me Mike Harker was a failed actor.'

'But that isn't him,' Trevor said through gritted teeth.

'Well, he's the man who turned up on my doorstep. This—I just don't understand. I danced with a dozen men.'

'Like *that?*' Trevor demanded, jabbing his finger at the picture. Jennifer drew a sharp breath as she saw what he meant. It had been taken at the moment when Steven had kissed her, and her response left no doubt about the matter. This was far from being just another dance.

She studied herself in dismay, her mind rejecting what her flesh remembered to be true. How could she have melted into his arms in that abandoned way?

And him? Had he too been lost? Or was he laughing

at a successful deception? And later— But she refused to remember later.

'I think I'd better have a talk to Mr Harker—or Leary, or whatever his name is,' she said grimly.

She called Charteris Enterprises. But she was stone-walled by Steven's secretary.

'Kindly tell Mr Leary that I don't know what his game is,' she said at last, 'but I'm going to find out.'

Steven had arrived at work to find the newspaper laid out on his desk and his staff ecstatic over his supposed coup. They'd known that Steven was negotiating to buy Kirkson Depots, a firm that operated in the same area as Nortons, but Kirkson was holding out for too high a price, and everyone now assumed that Steven had been playing a deep game.

He studied the picture, noticing how the clinging dress outlined Jennifer's splendid curves. She was looking up at him, her head thrown back in an attitude of ecstatic surrender, as though her partner was the only man in the world.

She'd wanted him to believe it was all an act, for the benefit of another man, and he'd been almost fooled— until the evening's final moments. Then the seductive spell she'd cast had swept him up. And not just him. She could deny it as much as she liked. He knew.

Alice, his secretary, looked in. She was thin, middle-aged and efficient. She also had a dry sense of humour that helped her survive as Steven's secretary. 'James Kirkson is here,' she said.

James Kirkson had come uttering words like 'compromise' and 'rethink'. Steven kept his face blank to conceal his sense of triumph. In another few minutes

Kirkson Depots would be his at a bargain price. But he was interrupted by the phone.

'It's Ms Norton,' Alice informed him. 'She's very cross and she's on her way here.'

Steven glanced at Kirkson and made a sudden decision. 'When she arrives,' he announced in a loud voice, 'tell her I love her madly.'

'Very good, sir.'

Exactly fifteen minutes later Alice's door burst open and Jennifer whirled in.

'I'd like to see Steven Leary,' she said crisply.

'I'm afraid that's not possible. Won't you sit down?'

'I won't be here long enough to sit down. Your employer is a devious, conniving—'

'You must be Ms Norton.'

'I certainly am.'

'In that case, Mr Leary loves you madly,' Alice declared, at her most wooden.

For a moment Jennifer felt as though something had knocked the wind out of her. Her head swam, the world glittered, shooting stars rioted in space. Then her senses cleared and she realised that Steven was up to his tricks.

'Does he employ you to talk that stuff?' she asked through twitching lips.

'On this occasion, yes.'

'Whatever he's paying you, it isn't enough.'

'I agree. Can I get you some coffee?'

'What you can get me is Steven Leary's head on a plate,' Jennifer said crisply. 'Better still, I'll collect it myself.'

Alice moved, but she wasn't fast enough. Jennifer swept into Steven's office, already uttering the words, 'How dare you tell the press all that rubbish about us when you know perfectly well—!'

She got no further. Steven was out of his chair and across the room in time to cut off the rest. His mouth descended on hers in mid-word. His arms were like steel about her, preventing all struggle.

Jennifer's indignation fought with her instinctive response. The sense of sheer power holding her exhilarated her even while it made her furious.

He released her mouth just long enough to say, 'Business *and* pleasure, darling.' Lowering his voice, he said urgently, 'Kiss me back, for pity's sake!'

'Not in a million years—' She barely got the words out before he silenced her again. The world spun around her, making it impossible to think, or do anything except feel a fierce, sensual delight deep inside her. It was stronger than anger. For a blinding moment it was the only thing in the world.

But the moment passed and she was herself again. She freed her lips, feeling her heart pounding, hoping she wasn't too flushed. She looked into his face, expecting to find in it a look of jeering triumph, and was astonished to see an echo of her own reaction. Steven was breathing hard and his eyes were glittering.

'Jennifer,' he said in a husky voice, 'let me introduce you to—where is he?'

'Mr Kirkson slipped out while you were occupied,' Alice informed him, from the doorway.

'Damn!' Steven said explosively, releasing Jennifer with unloverlike haste. 'He was on the verge of caving in.' He glared at Jennifer. 'Thanks a lot!'

'Are you daring to blame me?'

'If you hadn't barged in just then I could have bought Kirkson's for a knock-down price.'

'Kirkson Depots? So that was it all the time! You set me up last night.'

'No way. It was an accident.'

'Ho-ho-ho!' Jennifer scoffed.

'Don't you "ho-ho" me. You have a lot to answer for.'

'I—?'

'You've just wrecked a deal that would have made this firm a lot of money.'

'A deal that you wouldn't have been in a position to make if you hadn't deceived me.'

'I did not deceive you,' Steven said through gritted teeth. 'Mike Harker's a friend of mine. He was half-dead from flu, so I took his place. That's all.'

Alice looked in again. 'There's a call for Ms Norton. I've put it through.'

Puzzled, Jennifer picked up the phone on Steven's desk, and found herself talking to her brother. 'Trust you to dash off like that without stopping to think!' he complained. 'Barney called. He's over the moon about the rise in our share price.'

'Oh, no!' she breathed. Ever since the firm had gone public it had been Barney's dream to see the price rise, and now it had happened. How could she tell him that it was all an illusion?

'He wants you to bring Steven Leary to dinner.'

'Now see what you've started,' Jennifer said to Steven. 'My grandfather wants you to come to dinner.'

'Fine! I accept.'

'And then this crazy story will get another head of steam. Where will it end?'

'Who knows?' he said wickedly. 'But it might be interesting to find out.' He took the receiver from her. 'Mr Norton, I'd be delighted to accept your invitation.'

Jennifer lifted the extension in time to hear Trevor say, 'My grandfather has invited us all to his house the day after tomorrow. He asks me to say that he hopes you won't mind being outnumbered.'

'I could bring my sister, to even up the numbers and protect me,' Steven suggested.

'Naturally we should be delighted to entertain your sister, Mr Leary, if you think she won't be bored.'

'Maud is a very serious person,' Steven said in a grave voice. 'She's dedicated to making money. I'm sure that you and she will get on well.'

'I'll leave Jennifer to arrange the details with you.' Trevor hung up.

Meeting Jennifer's indignant gaze, Steven said, 'I'm looking forward to meeting your family properly. I'll tell my sister.'

'Barney likes to start the evening at eight,' Jennifer said formally.

'We'll be there at eight. By the way, didn't you notice that I won our bet? I said you'd contact me in less than a week.'

'But you knew this was bound to happen. That's cheating.'

'You owe me. Pay up.'

'Certainly not.'

'I wonder if the press knows how Nortons treats its debts of honour?' Steven mused to nobody in particular.

The teasing gleam in his eye checked Jennifer's retort. She took a deep breath. She knew she ought to escape as a matter of sheer self preservation, but after all it *was* a debt of honour.

'Very well,' she said, trying to speak calmly. 'You may kiss me for precisely five seconds.'

'Oh, I don't think we need to drag it out that long,' he said, dropping a peck on her cheek. 'There. Now you can slap my face if you like.'

'What I would like to do is something for which there are no polite words. When I think of your behaviour last night—letting me think you were just an impoverished actor when all the time—and you took those cufflinks under false pretences. I think you should return them.'

'No can do. I passed them on to the real Mike Harker, with your message about the price he could get for them.'

'It's time for me to go,' Jennifer said, speaking with difficulty. 'I will see you at dinner.'

'I'll look forward to it.'

It was the merest chance that took Steven past Jennifer's house the following evening. He'd been calling on a valuable client, or he wouldn't have been in that direction.

It seemed a good idea to drop in on her. It would be interesting to see her in what he thought of as more 'normal' circumstances. It would be even more interesting to catch her off guard. It was a moot point which motive was the stronger, but since he was honest with himself he admitted he would enjoy taking her by surprise.

But fate turned the tables on him, because whatever welcome he'd expected it wasn't the one he got.

His ring at the doorbell brought the sound of feet scurrying urgently. The next moment the door was yanked open and Jennifer stood there, gabbling with relief.

'Thank heavens you're here, I was getting so worried. I don't think there's much time—oh, dear, it's only you!'

Women had greeted Steven in a variety of ways, ranging from 'Darling, how wonderful!' to 'How dare you show your face here again?' But 'Oh, dear, it's only you,' was new to him.

'Yes, it's me,' he said. 'I gather I'm not who you were hoping to see?'

Without answering she darted past him, down the garden path and into the street. She looked up and down, then, failing to see what she was looking for, did a little dance of frustration.

Steven barely knew her. She was dressed in old jeans and a shapeless shirt that concealed everything he'd hoped to see again. Except for her legs. She had the longest legs of any woman he'd seen, and the shabby denim that covered them couldn't entirely disguise their beauty.

Her face was bare of make-up. Her hair hung free and looked as if she'd been running worried hands through it. A greater contrast to the elegant woman of the banquet or the avenging angel who'd whirled into his office could hardly be imagined.

'This is terrible,' she wailed as she returned to the house and shut the door.

'Thanks,' he said, slightly nettled. 'I'm sorry I'm such a disaster.'

'It's not your fault,' she said, tearing her hair. It flopped over her forehead. She shoved it back but it flopped again.

'Who did you hope I was?' he asked.

'The vet,' she said frantically. 'Paws has just gone into labour.'

'Paws—?'

'My cat. At least, she isn't actually mine, but she wandered in and took over, and I didn't know she was pregnant, but she started acting strangely and I suddenly realised how fat she was—'

'Whoa! I can't keep up. What do you mean, "acting strangely"?'

'She keeps digging holes in the garden and trying to settle into them, and she's panting, as if she's in pain.'

'Where is she?'

'I managed to get her back into her box in the front room.'

He followed her pointing finger to where the cat was curled up in large cardboard box lined with cushions. Paws regarded him anxiously, and he dropped down beside her, feeling her abdomen gently.

'Yes, she's got at least four in there, I should say,' he agreed.

'You know about cats?' she asked hopefully.

'When I was a kid our neighbour had a moggie who littered every six months. For some reason she always came to our garden to give birth, so I got quite used to it. She always preferred newspaper.'

'Right.' Jennifer dived into the kitchen and returned with a stack of papers. Steven gently lifted Paws out into Jennifer's arms, removed the cushions and lined the box thickly with paper. When Paws was returned she sniffed around, then settled down, purring and looking up at Steven with a trusting expression.

'You know what she's thinking, don't you?' Jennifer said with a shaky smile. ''Thank goodness for someone who knows what he's doing!''

'As long as she's satisfied. But I'd be happier if you had a proper vet.'

'He should have been here ages ago. That's who I thought you were. Can you keep an eye on her while I call and see what's happened to him?' She vanished before he could answer.

'She's crazy,' Steven confided to Paws. 'How could she not have noticed that you're expecting? Hey, you're in a bad way.'

The cat was panting again, quick shallow breaths of distress, while a look of fierce concentration came over her face.

'Tell them to hurry up,' Steven called.

But Jennifer was finding the crisis growing deeper every moment. 'Nobody knows where he is,' she said, returning to the front room. 'He left the surgery half an hour ago so he should have been here by now, but he seems to have vanished into thin air—is Paws eating a sausage?'

'No, that's a kitten,' Steven said. 'It was born a minute ago. She's licking it to get it breathing properly.'

Paws's pink tongue was working quickly over a minute black object that wriggled and emitted tiny squeaks. Jennifer dropped to her knees with a smile of delight, and stretched out a tentative hand to scratch Paws's head.

Steven quietly rose and went into the kitchen, returning in a few minutes with a pot of coffee. Jennifer was still leaning over the box, so rapt that she didn't notice him, and he had a moment to notice the soft light on her face as she watched with breathless excitement.

'I should leave her for a bit,' he suggested. 'She's barely started the job yet. She needs peace and quiet.'

He helped her to her feet and drew forward a couple of armchairs so that they shielded the box. 'That'll give her the feeling of privacy.'

'When did you do this?' Jennifer asked, looking at the coffee.

'I've been blundering my way around your kitchen. It wasn't easy, but I finally twigged that tea is in the sugar canister, sugar's in the garlic tin and coffee's in the container marked ''Tea''. Finding biscuits in the biscuit tin threw me a bit, but I coped.'

He poured the coffee and set the sugar near her with practised gestures. 'I'm very domesticated,' he said, noticing her glance. 'My mother saw to that.'

'It's somehow the last thing I'd have expected of you.'

'It's fatal to judge by appearances. I guess we both know that. I never expected to find you the way you are.'

'What did you expect to find? I mean, why are you here?'

'I'm not quite sure. I had to see a client out of town, and the way home lay in this direction. I dropped in on impulse, and got the surprise of my life.' He saw her trying to peek around the armchairs.

'Leave her,' he said firmly. 'It'll be half an hour before the next one's born. By that time, with any luck, the vet will be here.'

But half an hour came and went with no sign of the vet. Another kitten appeared. Steven felt Paws's abdomen gently, and said, 'Two more to come, but things are going well.'

'I'll make a spot of supper,' Jennifer said. 'It's the least I can do for you.'

She went into the kitchen and set to work. Steven looked around at her home, trying to reconcile it with his previous picture of her. When he'd first come here the other night he'd been puzzled to find her living in a bungalow. A smart little flat would surely have fitted the elegant creature in the figure-hugging dress? There had been a sophistication about her that pulled against the cosiness of this little villa. He wondered if somebody had left it to her.

'How long have you lived here?' he asked, lounging against the kitchen doorframe.

She looked up from rummaging in a cupboard. 'I bought it a couple of years ago.'

'Were you living with someone?'

'I beg your pardon?'

'I mean a bungalow is a strange choice for a woman on her own.'

'Is it?' She seemed surprised. 'I just loved this place the moment I saw it. I knew I had to live here.'

She began slicing up peppers. Steven watched her for a moment before turning back to the room. Jennifer heard him murmuring to Paws, and realised that there was no easy way of understanding this man.

In the last two days she'd researched him, and come up with tantalisingly little. He'd built up a chain of small shops before selling them off and joining Charteris Enterprises ten years ago. Charteris was a huge firm that had been underperforming. He'd turned it around, cutting out dead wood, selling off some sections, and doubling profits.

Jennifer had formed the impression of a man dedicated to business: a hard man, keen, ambitious, his mind totally focused on his ends. One newspaper item had hinted at a succession of female companions, none of whom lasted long, but apart from that there was little to suggest that he had a personal life. Wheeling and dealing seemed to be his absorbing passion.

But how did that predator tie up with the man acting midwife to her cat tonight? She was becoming more curious by the moment.

Steven's curiosity was also growing. The more he found the less he seemed to know. On the mantelpiece was a photograph of an elderly man with a thin, pixie face. Next to it was a picture of a boy and girl, both in their teens, and one of a woman in her thirties who bore a marked resemblance to Jennifer.

'That was my mother,' Jennifer said, entering with cutlery and starting to lay the table.

'Where's your father?'

'The old man on the end is my grandfather. You'll meet him tomorrow night.'

'I guessed that might be him. What about your father?'

'This one is Trevor and me together when we were kids.'

'Where—?'

Jennifer had vanished back into the kitchen.

When she returned with food some minutes later Steven had turned out all the lights except a small table-lamp, and was kneeling down beside Paws, murmuring, 'That's it—clever girl—not long now.' He heard Jennifer and looked up. 'She's happier in dim light. Can you see what you're doing?'

'Just about. Don't worry.'

She set rolls and salad on the table, and went to fetch the steaks. Steven positioned his chair where he could take discreet glances at Paws without bothering her.

The phone rang. Jennifer snatched it up and found herself talking to the vet.

'I'm really sorry,' he said. 'My car's broken down, and it'll be at least an hour before I'm there.'

'Don't worry,' Jennifer reassured him. 'She's in good hands.'

'Thanks for the vote of confidence,' Steven said wryly.

'She's all right, isn't she?' Jennifer asked anxiously.

'Doing fine, as far as I can tell. She really means a lot to you, doesn't she?'

'Well, she's such a sweet little thing.'

'And she's your only companion in this empty place?'

'I told you: I love it here.'

'Are you and David going to live here when you're married?'

'I think we'd better keep off the subject of David.'

'Has he been in touch since the other night?'

'I said that's enough,' Jennifer told him with a warning in her voice.

'I guess he hasn't.'

Jennifer refused to answer. She wasn't going to antagonise him, for Paws's sake, but he'd touched a nerve. There had been no sign from David.

'Can I have some more salad?' Steven asked meekly.

'Certainly,' Jennifer said in a frosty tone.

'Go on,' he dared her with a wicked grin. 'Give in to your feelings. Chuck it over me.'

'The only thing I feel towards you at this moment is gratitude on Paws's behalf,' Jennifer said primly.

'You really do love that cat if you're prepared to forgive me for mentioning David.'

'Can we change the subject now?'

'All right. Tell me why there are no photographs of your father.'

'Because he walked out when I was ten years old and nobody's heard from him since,' Jennifer said flatly.

'I see. I'm sorry. It's none of my business. But I don't understand. I thought I knew about Barney Norton, but I never heard he had a son.'

'He didn't. My mother was his daughter, his only child.'

'Then how come your name is Norton?'

'It used to be Wesley, but when our mother died Barney took us in and changed our names to his.'

'Did he ask you first?'

'No, he just did it.'

'Didn't you mind that?'

'Not at all. Have some more coffee.'

She'd changed the subject on purpose. She found her-self liking Steven now a lot more than she would have thought possible, but she couldn't have described to him the sensations of her teen self at gaining a new identity.

Jennifer Norton was Barney Norton's granddaughter, loved and wanted and sure of where she belonged in the world. Jennifer Wesley had been the girl who'd thought she was her father's pet until he'd dumped her without a backward glance. She'd cried through long nights for a betrayal she couldn't understand, for a wound that would never completely heal. No, she didn't want to be Jennifer Wesley again.

A glance at the clock told her that it was just the time David had used to call her. But that seemed a long time ago now.

The phone shrilled.

She was out of her chair and hurrying to answer with a speed that brought a frown to Steven's eyes. Watching her face, he saw how hope died as she heard the voice on the other end and it wasn't David's.

'I see,' she said brightly. 'Thank you for letting me know.'

She hung up and stood for a moment, coming to terms with the bleak emptiness inside. Whenever the phone rang it was always David—until it wasn't, and she be-came again the little girl who couldn't believe Daddy had gone for good because that was his key in the lock. But it was never him.

She saw Steven watching her and summoned up a

smile. 'That was the vet again, saying he's still trying to get here.'

'I see,' he said gently.

'Why are you staring at me?'

'Was I? I'm sorry. Let's have another look at the proud mother.'

Paws had produced a third kitten, and was about to have the fourth.

'I always made some warm milk about now,' Steven observed. 'After all that effort she needs something.'

'Warm milk,' she muttered, racing for the kitchen.

But the time she returned the fourth kitten had been born, and Paws was licking it vigorously. When she'd finished she accepted the milk, then settled down with a satisfied air of having done a hard job well.

'I think that's all,' Steven said, 'but it'll need the vet to be sure.'

'Look,' Jennifer said excitedly, 'the last one's got black fur and white paws, just like its mother.

'Paws Two,' Steven said with a grin.

'Maybe it's a boy. Then I ought to call him Steven.'

She sat down on the floor with her ankles crossed, gazing into the basket with an expression of total rapture.

'You stay there,' Steven said. 'I'll make coffee.'

'Uhuh!' was all the answer he received. Jennifer didn't mean to be impolite, but she was totally absorbed by the miracle. Steven crept away.

When he returned she was still in the same position, watching the new little family with delight. Steven regarded her, puzzled.

'This is what you really want to do, isn't it?' he asked, speaking almost in a whisper, so not to disturb the cats. 'Look after animals?'

'I suppose it is,' she said, accepting the coffee, and

also speaking in a whisper. 'Trevor says this place looks like a sanctuary sometimes, but I can't have too many animals because I'm away all day.'

'Being a tycoon.'

She made a face. 'I don't feel like a tycoon.'

'You don't look like one right now. Is this the woman who whirled into my office yesterday and told my secretary she wanted my head on a plate?'

Jennifer covered her eyes. 'Don't remind me of that when you've been so good to me.'

'But I love it. Alice says you sounded like a medieval tyrant saying, ''Bring me the head of Steven Leary.'''

'What I actually said was I'd collect it myself.'

'I wish I'd heard you,' he said with a grin.

'Steven, this is terrible. Officially I'm still mad at you for keeping me in the dark the other night.'

'That's OK,' he said with a grin. 'My back is broad.'

'But how can I be mad at you when I've just named a kitten after you?' she demanded logically.

'It's a puzzler, isn't it? Why don't you just change the kitten's name? Then we can be enemies again.'

'Do you want to be enemies?'

'It can be just as interesting as being lovers.'

'Friends, you mean.'

'I know what I mean.' His eyes were gleaming in the semi-darkness. Jennifer refused to rise to the bait.

'I shall never think of you as an enemy after tonight,' she said.

'Rash words. You don't know me well enough to be sure of that.'

'I suppose not. I probably never will.'

'With half London talking about our mad passion for each other?' he teased.

'They'll soon talk about something else. Scandals come and go.'

'Is that what we are? A scandal?'

'Food for the gossips,' she said firmly. 'They'll lose interest.'

'But will we?'

She knew they were straying into dangerous territory, but it was fascinating to sit here in the dim light, watching the gleam in his eyes. Of all the crazy ways to spend an evening!

And yet it was one of the nicest evenings she'd ever known. For all his flirtatious talk, her chief feeling was contentment. It was totally different from the dangerous sensations he'd inspired in her before, but just now it was what she needed.

The doorbell came as an unwelcome interruption. The vet stood there, apologising. Jennifer made the necessary replies and showed him indoors, to the box. Steven had already risen and was getting his things together. The pleasant evening was over.

'I'll see you tomorrow night, at your grandfather's house,' Steven said, making his way to the door. 'I'm looking forward to it, although I doubt if it'll be as interesting as tonight. Goodnight, Jennifer.'

'Goodnight, Steven. And thank you.'

CHAPTER FOUR

THE next day Jennifer spent the afternoon visiting a customer. She returned to her office to find a sheaf of telephone messages.

'David Conner called five times,' her secretary said. 'I don't think he believed me when I kept saying you were out.'

Since the banquet she'd thought a lot about David, wondering how he'd felt at seeing her. She'd resisted the temptation to call him on some pretext, and now her patience had been rewarded.

'David?' she said when he came on the line.

'Thank you for getting back to me, at last.' He spoke lightly, but with a slightly aggrieved note.

'I've been out. But I'm here now.'

'I thought we might have a drink, in our usual place.'

She hesitated. Steven and his sister were coming tonight, and she mustn't be late. 'It'll have to be a quick one.'

'Rushing off to a date?'

Her heart leapt. He minded. 'Of course not. I just have to get home.'

'The Crown, just for a few minutes.'

An hour later she slipped into The Crown, the softly lit cocktail bar where they'd often met before. It had worked. David wanted her back. Once tonight's dinner was over she could quietly disentangle herself from Steven.

David was at their usual table in the corner. He smiled

as she approached, giving her the gentle, uncertain look that always touched her heart. He stood to greet her and kissed her on the lips, but so quickly that she had no time to feel any thrill. There would be time for that later, she told herself.

They made small talk for a few minutes, avoiding both their quarrel and their last meeting. At last David said, 'Thank you for coming. I was afraid you weren't talking to me. I said a few things, that time, that were out of line.'

'I've forgotten it,' she said, smiling with happiness at being with him again.

'Have you? Isn't that why you were giving me the cold shoulder today?'

'David, I was out.'

'Sure that wasn't an excuse to avoid me?' he asked quietly.

'It was nothing to do with you.'

He gave a wry, disbelieving smile. For the first time Jennifer discovered that she could be irritated with David. His need for reassurance could be charming, but did he, perhaps, overdo it a little?

Steven's voice spoke in her head. *He looks the kind of self-centred idiot who thinks all roads lead back to him.* She bade the voice be silent.

'Honestly, David, I wasn't avoiding you. Our row's over and done with.'

'Of course. And you're sure you didn't tell your secretary to put me off?'

'I promise I didn't.'

'I wondered if I might be an embarrassment, now you've found someone else?'

He was jealous, she thought. He still loved her.

'*You've* found someone else yourself,' she said in a teasing voice, but inwardly agog for his answer.

'Penny? She's my secretary. She was just helping me out for the evening. You really pulled off a coup, arriving with Steven Leary.'

'You know him?'

'No—that is, I didn't know who he was that night, but since then one or two people have told me about him—'

He'd been asking about Steven. Heaven!

'You must be pretty close to have given him those cufflinks,' David observed.

She'd bought the cufflinks because David had admired them in a shop window. Obviously he'd recognised them. But she couldn't explain without revealing that she'd hired an escort, which she didn't want to do. While she was hesitating her mobile rang. It was Trevor.

'Where are you?' he demanded.

'Just having a quick drink. I'll be leaving directly.'

'I hope you hurry up. You know we have to get to Barney's for that Leary fellow.'

Trevor's hectoring voice carried. David stiffened and set down his drink. Jennifer hurriedly ended the call.

'I see,' David said heavily.

'It's not what you think. He and his sister are having dinner with us tonight.'

'How cosy.'

'It's just business, David.'

'Really?' he asked quizzically.

'Really. I must go now.'

He held her hand briefly and their eyes met. She leaned down to kiss him, enjoying the warm, comforting touch of his lips. How often in the last few weeks had she longed for it? Now it was hers again.

As David released her she had an odd sense of something missing, something that should have happened and hadn't. But it was foolish to judge David's kisses by Steven's. No one man kissed like any other, and this was her David, whom she loved. She pulled herself together.

'Goodbye, darling,' she said.

'Goodbye. Have a nice evening.'

'Without you?' she asked lightly. 'How could I?'

He smiled and brushed the back of her hand with his lips. Jennifer left with a light heart. She was a little surprised that he hadn't asked to see her again, but she decided that was probably because she'd hurried away before he'd had the chance.

Barney's house was a mansion on the edge of London. Jennifer reached it with enough time to bathe and dress for dinner. As she relaxed in the bath she glanced at the local paper that she'd found in the hall, and something she found there made her eyes open wide.

The gown she'd chosen was olive-green and coolly sophisticated, with a modest neckline just low enough for a simple gold chain, from which hung a garnet. More garnets glowed in her ears. She was triumphant with happiness that her estrangement from David was over, and that he cared enough to be jealous.

She went downstairs to find Trevor there, smartly and soberly attired, his stocky frame radiating gravity. He nodded approval at his sister's appearance.

'I'm glad I've got you alone for a moment,' she said quietly, handing him the local paper. 'Did you see this?'

'"Man fined for being drunk and disorderly",' Trevor read. 'What's so special about that?'

'Look at the name.'

He did so, then whistled. 'Fred Wesley!'

'Our father's name,' Jennifer reminded him.

'Probably just a coincidence. There must be a lot of Fred Wesleys in the world.'

'Suppose it isn't? Suppose he's hanging around here?'

'Jennifer, we haven't heard of him for years. We don't even know if he's alive. And we certainly don't want him turning up again.'

'Don't we?'

'You were too young to know what was going on, but he was bad news. According to Barney, he went after Mum because she had a rich father, and got her pregnant on purpose. When they were married he played around and lived off the money Barney supplied. I heard the rows. Know what he said to me once? "When you grow up, son, never forget that the world is full of women." I was fourteen. A week later Barney cut off the money and told him to get a job. So he moved out to live with his latest bit of fluff. Believe me, we don't want him back.'

'No, I suppose not,' Jennifer mused. She knew what Trevor said was true. Young as she'd been, she too had heard a lot of the rows. She gave herself a little shake. It was morbid thinking this way, and she wanted her wits about her this evening. But she couldn't resist asking, 'Did you ever learn Dad's lesson?'

'About what?'

'The world is full of women.'

'I've had a job to do,' Trevor replied austerely. 'It hasn't left time for the kind of liaisons our father regarded as normal.'

'Yes, you seem to have reacted against him and become a puritan,' she said with a touch of mischief. 'Dad would probably be ashamed of you.'

'I hope so. I'm certainly ashamed of him. I hope our guests aren't going to be late.'

'I wonder what Mr Leary's sister is like?' Jennifer mused.

'A businesswoman, according to him. Besides, her name is Maud.'

'What's that got to do with it?'

'There's something in the name Maud that inspires confidence,' Trevor said, in a voice that settled the matter for all time.

Upon reflection, Jennifer had to agree that he was right.

Barney appeared, dressed to kill. For a man who'd once been so formidable his physique was unimpressive. He was barely five feet six inches, and built on frail lines. His hair was white and thinning rapidly, his face was long and mild, and his eyes genial. A stroke, five years ago, had left him with a limp and an impaired memory. Only the gentle, kindly side of his nature was left, and tonight his eyes were gleaming with enjoyment at the prospect of a dinner party.

Right on cue the bell rang. Jennifer opened the door to find Steven standing there.

'Good evening, Mr Leary.'

'Good evening, Miss Norton.' His tone was admirably formal, but the gleam in his eye belonged to a pirate. 'May I introduce my sister, Maud?'

He stood aside, giving everyone a clear view of the young woman with him. There was a moment's stunned silence.

Maud Leary was in her mid-twenties and haughtily beautiful, in the style of an Afghan hound. Her height nearly equalled her brother's, although it was exaggerated by the way she wore her hair, pulled back from her face and drawn high up into a ponytail on the very top of her head. From there it fell halfway down her back.

Her floor-length dress was in the Grecian style, gathered under the bust and falling straight to the ground. It seemed to be made of metallic gauze, through which could be seen her slim, elegant form, apparently clad in nothing else, although Jennifer noticed the flesh-coloured body stocking.

Trevor drew a sharp breath. Glassy-eyed, he moved forward to greet the apparition, and found himself holding a gold-taloned hand, pointing down, as though its owner expected him to kiss it.

'How do you do?' he said hoarsely.

'How do you do?' she responded in a husky voice.

Steven met Jennifer's eyes and she smiled back, sharing his amusement. 'I can see it's going to be quite an evening,' she said in a low voice.

Steven grinned. 'I wonder if I was right to bring Maud.'

'You think he'll bore her?'

'No, I'm afraid she may eat him alive. It's her hobby.'

'Don't worry about Trevor. Nothing gets to him. How does she come to look so marvellous?'

'By devoting her life to it. She's a model.'

'You told Trevor she was dedicated to business.'

'No, I said dedicated to making money. She earns a fortune.'

'You know that's not how you made her sound.'

Steven's grin made his face suddenly delightful. 'I couldn't help it. Your brother's such a pompous ass that I'm afraid he brought out the worst in me. I'm sorry if that offends you.'

Jennifer laughed. 'It doesn't. I must admit, I've often thought the same.'

'By the way, how are the new mother and babies?'

'In the pink of health. They turned out to be three girls and a boy, all flourishing. The vet was very pleased with how well Paws had come through it. I didn't get the chance to thank you properly.'

'No need. All I did was sit there.'

'But you knew what you were doing, and I think Paws knew that. It made her feel secure. I just made her nervous.'

'As long as she's all right.'

They moved in to dinner. Barney had placed Steven on one side of him and Jennifer on the other. To her dismay, Trevor was next to Maud. Whatever would they talk about? she wondered.

But when she next looked they seemed to be absorbed in each other. Trevor was talking earnestly and Maud was answering in monosyllables. Jennifer caught snatches of his words: 'market share…forward price… Dow-Jones index…' Maud's huge eyes were fixed intently on his face, but it was impossible to tell if there was anything behind them. To Jennifer they looked totally vacant.

She turned her attention back to Steven and discovered him deep in conversation with Barney. They were sitting at right angles to the table, which made it easy for her to follow.

'You didn't know it, sir, but you were my mentor,' Steven was saying. 'When I was studying business there was one lecturer who took your career as a template. He knew every deal you'd ever made, and he analysed them all: all your sharp moves and the other guys' mistakes— which were mostly taking your words at face value.'

Barney roared with laughter. He was thoroughly enjoying himself, and Jennifer could see that he and Steven had recognised each other as kindred spirits.

The conversation became general. Trevor, incredibly for him, told a funny story about Jennifer's first days in the firm, and her early mistakes.

'That's not fair,' she protested, amid laughter. 'I don't do that sort of thing any more.'

'You're worse,' Trevor said. 'You still act first and think later. We call it Jennifer's "red mist",' he explained to Maud. 'It overtakes her without warning and makes her do mad things that I have to spend days sorting out.'

'That's a slander,' Jennifer cried, but inwardly she was delighted to see her brother loosen up and actually smile. In fact he was smiling a lot, mostly in Maud's direction.

It was a warm night, and when dinner was over coffee and liqueurs were served outside on the patio. Trevor was still talking to a fervently listening Maud. Barney had settled down to his favourite subject: his garden.

'I'd like to show it to you, but I'm a little tired. Jennifer, dear, why don't you do the honours?'

Steven took up his glass, and handed one to Jennifer. 'Let's go,' he said.

The garden was dotted with cleverly placed floodlights in various colours, so despite the darkness they found their way along the winding paths among the trees.

'This is an enchanted place,' was Steven's unexpected remark. 'I have a large garden myself, and one day I'd like to do something like this with it. But for the moment Maud is the one who looks after it.'

'She lives with you?'

'Kind of. She travels so much on assignments that it

isn't worth her having her own place, so she keeps a couple of rooms in my house.' He caught a fleeting expression on her face and added quickly, 'And if you're thinking that I come the heavy-handed brother, forget it. Maud looks like the fairy on the Christmas tree, but she's as tough as old boots.'

'I believe models need to be. They're also used to coping with boredom, aren't they?' Jennifer gave a chuckle. 'I expect that's coming in very handy just now.'

'I doubt if anything has prepared her for Trevor,' he agreed.

They drifted lazily along the half-lit paths towards the ornamental pond. It was long and narrow, with a rustic, lamplit bridge over the centre. Jennifer leaned over the railing, looking into her wine glass, listening to the sleepy grunts of the ducks below.

'I have the feeling David Conner has called,' Steven said suddenly.

'You're guessing.' She tried to sound cool, but she couldn't help the smile that touched her lips. Steven was watching her closely.

'I know that you're completely different tonight,' he said. 'The first time we met you were tense and uneasy. The second time you were hopping mad. Last night you were nice, but distracted. Now you're happy and charming. The reason's obvious.'

'Maybe.' She raised her glass in an ironic toast, not even realising that her eyes, gazing at him over the rim, were provocative.

'You shouldn't look at a man like that if you don't mean it,' Steven told her.

'I was only toasting your astuteness. You seem to be able to read me pretty well.'

'Not everything. I can't understand about Conner.

What does he have that transforms you from a nervous witch into a seductive siren?'

'So you think I'm a seductive siren?' she mused, laughing at him.

'You know what I think of you, Jennifer, just as I know that it's mutual. It's there despite the fact that we don't see eye to eye about a lot of things. It's there despite your lover. Is Conner your lover, by the way?'

The question caught her off guard. For the moment she was bereft of words, and Steven went on, 'I don't mean recently, since you quarrelled. Before that.'

'I won't discuss my love life with you—' she began.

'Seeing that you don't seem to have much of one that's a sensible decision. I'd like us to make love.'

His bluntness took her breath away. 'Well, we're not going to make love,' she managed to say.

'In a sense that's what we're doing right now, and you know it. Whatever we say on the surface, there's something else going on underneath, and it has to do with what we learned about each other that first night. Remember when we kissed goodnight? Can you leave it there? Because I can't.'

'You're wrong. David is all I could want. That's why I was heartbroken when I thought I'd lost him.'

'Yes, I remember some of the details of your—er— heartbreak,' Steven said wickedly. He eyed her indignant expression before observing, 'I believe this is the moment where you slap my face. Go ahead and get it over with— What's that?'

'Where?' she asked, trying to get her bearings after his abrupt change of subject.

'Over there.'

A murmur of voices came through the trees, and then

they saw two figures, one tall and willowy, the other broad and stocky, silhouetted by coloured lamps.

'Quick,' Steven said, seizing her hand and drawing her off the bridge into the shadows. Hidden by the trees, they watched as Trevor and Maud strolled over the bridge, Maud's hand held in Trevor's. His voice reached them. It was low, murmuring, intimate.

'Of course a referral to the Monopolies & Mergers Commission drives the share price down, and that's the time to buy, but only if…'

They passed on out of sight.

Steven and Jennifer stood in stunned silence. Then, in the same moment, they exploded into muffled laughter.

'I don't believe it,' she choked. 'Even of Trevor.'

Steven wiped his eyes. 'My poor Maud. She'll never forgive me for this.'

'Moonlight and flowers,' Jennifer said, going off into another gale of laughter. 'And all he can talk about is the Monopolies & Mergers Commission. Oh, heavens! I'll never be an aunt at this rate.'

The tension that had crackled between them was gone for the moment. Laughter had dissolved it into camaraderie—less thrilling, but just as pleasurable in its way. They began to walk on by the water, until they reached a rustic bench and sat there, watching the glow worms.

'I think it's time we discussed how to manage our separation carefully,' she said, 'so that nobody's shares dive.'

'Whoa, there! Who's talking about a separation yet?'

'But this can't go on.'

'It's not as simple as you think. We need to let people see us together at least once more. The day after tomorrow there's a shareholders' meeting for Dellacort Inc.

We've both got stock in the firm, so it'll be quite natural for us to attend together.'

'I don't know...' she mused.

'David is also a stockholder,' Steven said wickedly, 'so he'll probably be there. Think of the possibilities, Jennifer. He'll see us together, you'll tell him it's only business, while contriving, of course, to suggest that you're being evasive, and with any luck he'll send you roses that same evening.'

'You're too good at this,' Jennifer said.

'Manipulation is my middle name.'

His grin was irresistible, and Jennifer's lips twitched. 'Well, I was going to that meeting anyway,' she said. 'And if it has the right effect on David, I suppose I can help you out for a few more hours.'

'Jennifer,' he said admiringly, 'when you talk like that, no man could resist you.'

'Steven, I'll do one more thing, but that's it. Then we have to bring this to an end.'

'We'll see. I may have other ideas. Careful with your drink. You'll spill it on your dress, and that would be a pity, given the delightful way you're filling it out.'

'Don't change the subject.'

'Your charms *are* the subject, as far as I'm concerned. I lie awake dreaming about them. I've lost my appetite and become a shadow of my former self.'

'And pigs fly,' she said, meeting his teasing eyes. 'You're too full of yourself to lose food or sleep.'

'True,' he admitted, 'but I thought I'd say the right thing to show willing. And stop flirting with your eyes. I'm not David Conner, to be teased into delight.

Jennifer chuckled. She felt happy and self-confident. 'Think I couldn't delight you if I set my mind to it?'

'Only if I decided to let you.'

'I'm sure you've already made that decision. You're not a man to let the grass grow under his feet.'

He raised his glass, acknowledging a hit.

'Did you decide to "let" me the other night?' she asked.

'The other night I was acting a role.'

'Not all the time. I was the one acting, for David's benefit.'

'Including that subtle way you caressed my cheek on the side he couldn't see?'

'You imagined that,' she said quickly.

'I'm a man of no imagination whatever. And what about David's partner? Was she acting too?'

'She's his secretary: helping out was part of her duties.'

'But she's there with him all day, every day. Nine till five. Later, if she's very keen on her work. Yes sir, no sir, three bags full, sir. You should be worried.'

'I know David better than you do.'

'You know nothing about men at all, Jennifer, or you wouldn't have come out into a moonlit garden with me. You'd have known that I'd never let you depart unkissed.'

She'd known exactly that, of course, but pride made her say, 'I'm going back to the house now.'

'Not until you've kissed me. I want to know if I've remembered it right.'

Jennifer tried to tear her eyes away from his, but he seemed to hold her in thrall. Against her will she felt her memory calling up sensations she wanted to forget. They weren't touching, yet she could feel him kissing her as he'd done the other night. The heat was rising in her body now, just as then.

Abruptly she rose from the seat and walked on. He

followed her and caught up, taking her hand in his. 'Listen,' he said softly.

Jennifer listened, and heard the piercing sweet trill of a nightingale.

'If I was making love to you,' Steven murmured, 'I'd talk about you, and the things we both feel, even though you deny them, and I don't believe in them.'

'That doesn't make sense,' she told him, speaking slowly, for she felt as if she were in a dream. 'How can you feel things you don't believe in?'

'It's alarmingly easy. You give me feelings that I know don't exist. If I thought they did, I'd be scared. Even knowing that it's all an illusion—you trouble me, Jennifer.'

They'd reached a large oak tree. Jennifer leaned against the trunk and watched the moon and stars gleaming through the branches. The whole universe seemed to reel overhead, while the breeze softly rustled the leaves.

'Perhaps you should be worried anyway,' she mused softly. 'Some illusions are stronger than reality.'

'You feel that too?'

'But they don't last. You'll return to earth.'

'Will you?'

'I never left it,' she said, knowing herself to be a liar.

He leaned his broad shoulders against the trunk, and stood watching her. 'One of us is a great self-deceiver,' he said. 'I wonder which.'

'We'll probably never know.'

'We'll know one day. Let's hope it isn't too late when it happens.'

He put his hands against the trunk on each side of her head. His body was pressing against hers very slightly, effectively making her a prisoner. She smiled up at him, still feeling in command of the situation. As he began to lower his mouth to hers she was ready for him.

But then something happened. The world seem to shift, altering her perspective, making her wonder what she was doing here, playing love games, when the man she really loved was somewhere else. It was David, with his sweet nature and gentle smile, who held her heart, because she held his. She doubted if Steven Leary even had a heart to offer.

As his lips were about to touch hers she turned her head aside with a swift intake of breath. Steven stopped, regarding her through narrowed eyes. He saw the slight tremor of her mouth and the glint on her eyelashes, and he understood. Abruptly he moved away.

'You really don't know the first thing about men, do you?' he said harshly.

Jennifer was about to defend herself, but he was already walking away.

Since their parents had died, many years earlier, Steven and Maud had been each other's only family. Despite the fourteen-year difference in their ages, they confided in and relied on each other. Maud admired her brother's brains and he respected her shrewdness.

'So that's Jennifer,' she said on the way home. 'She's delightful. There's a sort of radiance about her.'

'Yes, there is,' he said slowly. 'One call from her lover and she's a different woman.'

'But aren't you her lover?'

'Not yet.' Steven said. He fell into a brooding silence, oblivious of the curious looks Maud was giving him.

'Who's the other man?' she asked at last.

'A nobody called David Conner. He won't last.'

'But he's there now, getting in your way,' Maud said

with a chuckle. 'This is going to be fun. I used to think you'd never meet your match.'

'And I never will. Jennifer's quite a woman, and I'm looking forward to the next few weeks. But I don't think I have much to worry about.'

'Brother dear,' Maud purred, 'I may not be clever about things. But I'm very, very clever about people.'

'I've never doubted it.'

'If there's going to be a battle, I'm backing her. I'd rather like to see you writhing in the toils of love.'

That made him laugh out loud. 'Don't count on it. By the way, I'm sorry about tonight. If I'd know what Trevor Norton was like I wouldn't have let you in for an evening with him.'

'Oh, but I thought he was perfectly sweet.'

'Sweet? That pompous, half-baked, hidebound—'

'Steven, please! Don't insult the man I'm going to marry.'

CHAPTER FIVE

As STEVEN had predicted, David was at the meeting. Jennifer saw him as she and Steven were leaving. She also saw Penny sitting beside David, who was laughing as though very well pleased with her company. The sight gave her a pang.

'Let's go and have lunch,' Steven said, squeezing her hand slightly.

The conference centre's restaurant was airy and spacious, with a glass roof that flooded the elegant grey decor with light. Steven led Jennifer to the best table in the place, beside a window where they had a view of a fountain display in a courtyard. A waiter held out a chair for her, but Steven waved him aside and manoeuvred her to the other side of the table. It was clear that he knew exactly what he wanted, down to the last detail. Jennifer found her own view of the other tables rather restricted, while Steven could see everything.

'I can't see,' she protested.

'Don't worry, I'll tell you everything you need to know about the saintly David.'

'Don't call him saintly.'

'I thought I was paying him a compliment.'

'You thought nothing of the kind. You wouldn't feel flattered if I called you saintly.'

'I've been called many names in an enjoyably misspent life, but saintly wasn't among them.' His eyes, full of meaning, were on her face. 'Certainly never from a woman. Hasn't it occurred to you that we might really give David cause for jealousy?'

'He's already jealous, thank you.'

'He doesn't look it. He's just walked in with Penny on his arm. Don't turn around. Remember, you're lost in the charm of my society.'

'Am I indeed?'

'If you want to get him back, yes. The waiter's showing him to a table—no! Conner's pointing to this part of the room—he wants to be where he can see us. That's encouraging.' He saw Jennifer's indignant glare. 'I'm only trying to be helpful,' he said blandly.

'I mistrust you most when you look innocent. Besides, I told you, he's already jealous.'

'How do you know? Did he come storming around to your home, threatening to put a bullet through us both if you ever saw me again?'

'Certainly not,' she said, laughing reluctantly.

'Then he threatened to put a bullet through himself? Yes, that's much more effective. Play on her heart, be a little pathetic. Works every time.'

'Surely that can't be experience talking?'

'I've never needed to employ pathos, and no woman has ever seen me at the end of my tether. But I've watched it done very effectively. All right, he hasn't thought of that one yet. I know—he threatened to ruin me financially?'

'David wouldn't kn—isn't that kind of man,' she corrected herself hastily.

'And he wouldn't know how,' Steven supplied. 'Exactly. All right, what *did* he do in his frenzy of jealous despair?'

'We met for a drink,' Jennifer said, wishing the words didn't sound so lame.

'And?'

'And what?'

'Don't stop just when it's getting interesting. What did he say? Or is it too intimate and passionate for my ears?'

'Quit trying to wind me up. Anyway, I told you all this the other night.'

'Do you mean we're still discussing that one little meeting?' he demanded, aghast. 'And there hasn't been another one since? My poor Jennifer! What did you do to get saddled with this booby? If I were in love with you, I'd have played merry hell by now.'

'How lucky for me that you're not!'

'Lucky for both of us if this is how you conduct a love affair. There's so much for me to teach you that I don't know where to start.'

'Don't bother. I can sort myself out with David without your help.'

'Fine, I'll come to your wedding—in about fifty years' time.'

'Perhaps he's just as you said—saintly?'

'What a bore he must be!'

'He's a gentleman, if that's what you mean.'

'Same difference!' He studied her for a moment. 'Do you know how lovely you are when your cheeks go that delicate pink?' He waited for her to answer, but she was determined not to.

'He's looking this way,' Steven said after a moment. 'He doesn't like seeing you with me any more than you like seeing him with Penny.'

'I don't give a rap about her; I keep telling you.'

'That's right. You keep telling me. He's turned away now. Their heads are together over the menu.'

'I don't wish to know that—'

'Kindly leave the stage,' he capped.

It was ridiculous. Jennifer tried to keep a straight face but she couldn't manage it.

'It's all right to laugh,' Steven said, watching her face appreciatively. 'Go on, give in to it. That's better.'

He could be disastrously charming when a certain gleam came into his eyes. Suddenly Jennifer was light-headed. The sun was shining on the fountains, the champagne glistened, and she was sitting with a wickedly attractive man who was giving her his whole attention. The thought danced through her head that she could easily become used to this.

Steven embarked on an anecdote about a mutual acquaintance. It was hilarious, and Jennifer rocked with laughter. He joined in and their eyes met. At once she knew it had been a mistake. He seemed to look deep into her, causing a feeling of agitation to start far down in her depths. It rose and spread until it pervaded her through and through. It glittered, too, like tinsel on a Christmas tree, so that her whole being was alive and joyful with the wonderful sensation.

Their lunch was served. She was vaguely aware that the food was delicious, but that sensation was lost in the greater pleasure of Steven's company. He focused his whole attention on her, as though nothing else existed in the world, and, although she knew that he was a clever man, and not to be trusted, she was flattered despite herself. Other women were staring at her with envy. The most attractive, dominant male in the room was absorbed in her, doing her honour, and the feeling was very sweet.

She caught him watching her with a half-smile, and raised her eyebrows in mute query.

'I'm admiring your power-dressing,' he explained, indicating her elegantly tailored charcoal business suit with the snowy white blouse and smart gold accessories.

'It's just as seductive as those daring evening gowns you wear, in a different way.'

'It's not meant to be seductive,' she said primly. 'It's meant to declare that I'm a serious mover in the commercial world.'

'And show off your legs,' he said irrepressibly.

She laughed, and ceded him the point. She was proud of her long legs, clad in dark silk tights that emphasised their perfect shape.

'And I'll bet your hands are manicured to perfection,' he went on. 'Let me see.'

'I wish you'd stop talking nonsense,' she said, but not too seriously, showing him her hand. He took it in his, and touched it with his lips.

'Gallantry from you is something I didn't expect,' she observed lightly.

'I'm acting as a good friend. David is glancing over here, wondering about us. He watches as I kiss the back of your hand—like this—but it doesn't worry him too much, because it's chivalrous, which he understands. But when I turn it over and kiss the palm—like this—then he starts to worry—rightly—because he knows my thoughts of you have taken another turn.'

Jennifer drew a soft, shuddering breath as his tongue flickered against her palm. Excitement raced along her nerves, pervading her whole body, making her heart begin to beat more powerfully and heat radiate out to her loins.

'He knows I want to undress you,' Steven murmured against her hand. 'He probably guesses that I've been thinking of it ever since the night we met.'

'Steven—' she said urgently.

'What he doesn't know is exactly how I'd do it—bit by bit, very slowly, savouring, enjoying every last second, and making sure you enjoyed it too. You would, you know.'

'You are insufferably arrogant,' she whispered, speaking with difficulty through the thunder in her ears.

'Why? Because I know I could make you enjoy sharing passion with me? Don't you think you would?'

She couldn't answer. She was fighting the seductive pictures his words conjured up. She knew that, just as he'd said, she *would* relish letting him undress her, very much indeed. Then perhaps she would undress him in return, and discover all the things about his body that were now so tantalisingly hidden. Were his shoulders as broad and his stomach really as flat as she suspected? Were his hips as lean and narrow as in her haunted imaginings, and his thighs as powerful? Would she ever find out the truth?

At the same time she felt a rising indignation at Steven. He could make her want what she'd decided not to want, and it was unforgivable of him. He knew that this was a meaningless flirtation and she really belonged to David, but he shamelessly used the situation to make her doubt herself.

No! She corrected that quickly. She had no doubts. Her true feelings were all for David, and this was only a passing madness. When it was over she would be a better wife for having got it out of her system. If only it could be over soon! If only it would last for ever!

'What are you thinking?' he asked.

'Nothing—very much,' she said, startled.

'You were a million miles away in some mysterious world of your own. And you won't let me in, will you?'

'No, I can't let you in.'

'Is *he* there?'

'I don't know,' she said with a touch of wistfulness.

'I thought I knew once—but things have changed between us—'

'Jennifer, don't look like that,' he said suddenly. 'Not for another man.'

'David isn't "another man". He's the one.'

'Then heaven help us both,' he said, so quietly that she almost didn't hear.

Dismayed, she saw what had happened. The conversation had started as deliciously seductive teasing, but in a few brief seconds it had swerved and taken them to the edge of a pit.

Hurriedly she began to back away, pouring another glass of mineral water for herself, then for him, praising the food, asking questions about nothing. He answered briefly, as though his mind was elsewhere. When she ventured to look up she found him watching her, not with the mockery she'd half expected, but like a man who'd been caught on the wrong foot. After that neither of them said very much.

When they left Steven offered her his arm and they made their progress from the restaurant, still attracting glances from all around. Jennifer's last view was of David, staring at her as though thunderstruck.

The annoying thing about Steven, Jennifer discovered, or rather, one of the *many* annoying things about him, was the way his most outrageous words lingered in her mind, casting their light over the events of her life.

It had been easy to laugh at his comical forecasts of David's jealous behaviour, but when two more days had passed without a word from him it stopped being funny. She was glad Steven wasn't there, ready with a cynical laugh or a jeering word.

That set her thinking about him, and then she realised

that she'd never really stopped thinking about him. At every turn he'd been present, sometimes giving her the predatory look that warned her that whatever he did was for himself. At other times she would remember what she'd seen on his face in the conference restaurant, and hear him mutter, 'Heaven help us both!' That troubled her most. Of course she was well armed against him, and yet the glint of his eyes seemed to cast a spell over her. If she hadn't been in love with David...

David telephoned her to say he would be away for a week. He'd had to hurry to the south coast, where his mother was ill. Luckily she was making a good recovery, and he would call Jennifer again when he returned.

Steven invited her to a show, and she accepted. It turned out to be a 'play of ideas', most of which made her cross. Steven was more in sympathy with the author's views, and over dinner afterwards they began a lively argument that continued all the way home. By the time they parted some extremely frank things had been said on both sides. Jennifer couldn't remember when she'd enjoyed herself so much.

He telephoned next day and they had a drink in the evening. But she made an excuse to leave early. The truth was that she enjoyed Steven's company too much, and the sooner this was brought to an end the better.

She seemed to be split in two, her reasonable mind arguing against her senses. It was madness to be involved with Steven, no matter how seductive he seemed. She knew what a relationship with him would offer: all the thrill and excitement of a fireworks display, an experience never to be forgotten.

But fireworks sparkled and died. Too soon the show would be over, the field cold and deserted and the audience left to trail home alone. The little girl who'd once been cold and deserted was still sufficiently alive in her to make her reject that choice. She wanted roots, a solid life, a long-time commitment. In other words, David.

She would get this far in her musings before remembering that David was conspicuous by his absence. Had he called her at that moment she would have been his for the asking.

Then she would remember Steven's teasing smile, with its hint of devilment, and warmth would begin to steal through her body until she was lost in her awareness of him, forgetful of everything else. She would awaken from these trances shocked and fearful, resolved to be strong and put him out of her life. But somehow it never happened.

At last David called and asked to see her in their little cocktail bar. It was genuinely difficult for her to manage, and she warned him she would be late, but he seemed anxious.

'I really do need to see you. I'll wait until you can make it.'

She just wished Steven could have witnessed her triumph.

David was at their usual table. He stretched out a hand at her approach. 'I was afraid you wouldn't come,' he said, closing his fingers over hers. 'And it's so important.'

'What's important, David?' she asked eagerly.

'Martson Engineering.'

'Martson—?'

'They're giving me the runaround, just as you said they would. I hate to admit it, but you were right all along.'

For a moment she couldn't think what he was talking

about. Then she remembered that their original quarrel had started with Martson.

'I guess I should have listened to your advice,' David admitted. 'I brought the correspondence along.'

The papers confirmed what she'd tried to warn David about weeks ago—clumsily, as she now told herself. For why else would he have taken offence?

Suddenly David said, a mite too casually, 'I saw you at the Dellacort meeting. It seems to be getting serious between you and Leary.'

'There's nothing between us,' she said quickly. 'Someone got the wrong idea about us at the banquet and wrote something that made the shares move up. I'm waiting for the right moment to drop him.'

'You mean that's all?'

'That's all.'

'That's not what—hang on a minute! There's a man over there who owes me some money. I've been trying to pin him down for days. I'll be back. Don't go away.'

He moved off. Jennifer sipped her mineral water, looking slowly around the room, and gradually became aware that an extremely handsome young man was edging towards her table, wearing a look of faint apprehension.

'Ms Norton?' he asked at last.

'I'm Jennifer Norton,' she agreed.

'I tried your office, but you'd gone, and your secretary said you often dropped in here. My name's Mike Harker.'

'Good heavens!' Jennifer exclaimed.

'I guess you think I've got a nerve—'

'No, I'm just amazed to discover that you actually exist. Sit down.'

'Thanks.' He took the seat beside her.

'Have you recovered from the flu?'

'Oh, Steven told you about that. I wasn't sure how much you knew.'

'I found out the truth next morning.'

'He only meant to do me a favour,' Mike urged. 'I was at my wits' end, and he'll do anything for a friend.'

'Did he tell you how the evening went?'

'No. He was laughing when he got back, but he wouldn't tell me what the joke was. Did he annoy you very much?'

'I'm not blaming you. And I haven't complained to the agency, if that's what's worrying you.'

'No, it's not that. It's these.' Mike reached into his pocket and laid the diamond cufflinks on the table. 'Of course I couldn't keep them.'

'Why not? I gave them to you, indirectly.'

'But you didn't mean to, and they're too valuable for me to accept.'

'Please do,' she said warmly. 'I don't make gifts and then take them back, even under the oddest circumstances. I can't believe that you went to these lengths to find me.'

'I've been treading on eggshells, not knowing what I'd find. But it's all right. You're with that guy over there, aren't you?'

'Yes, I am.' Light dawned. 'But, Mike, if you'd thought I was getting involved with Steven, what would you have wanted to warn me about?'

A grin broke over his face. 'Well, you've met Steven—'

'That's why I'm asking.'

'Let's just say I'm glad you're not involved with him. Not that I've seen much of him in the past few years, but I don't think he's changed.'

'You go back a long way?'

'We were at night school together. That's where he did his business studies. He was always "love 'em and leave 'em". No woman could pin him down and he was proud of that. So of course they were all lining up for him. Can't think why. I suppose you couldn't blame him for likening them to buses.'

'Buses?'

'Always another one along soon.'

'Is that what he says?' Jennifer asked, wide-eyed and innocent. 'Fancy.' She felt as though her insides were tying themselves in knots at the unfortunate echo of those words. 'I used to know another man who said something like that,' she mused. '"The world is full of women." That was how he put it, but I guess it means much the same.'

'I don't think Steven intended it very seriously,' Mike said. 'It was more like a game to him. I wouldn't have told you, but you've got someone else, so it's all right.'

'Perfectly all right.' Jennifer added invitingly, 'So you can tell me everything. Steven was a devil in those days, wasn't he?'

'I'll say. He could help himself to any female. Pity, really. Do him good to get a knock. Hell, I shouldn't say that, when he helped me out, but it can really get under your skin. He's so damned sure of himself.'

'Yes, he is,' Jennifer murmured. 'Well, he'll probably take a tumble one day, like everyone else.'

'Not if he can help it. Steven says no woman's so special that a man need make a fool of himself.'

'He says that, does he?' Jennifer leaned back into the shadows lest her face betray her reaction to this conversation. She discovered that she was drumming her fingers tensely and made herself stop. None of this should come as a surprise. She knew what Steven was like, and besides, David was the one she loved.

'We went to a wedding once,' Mike recalled. 'It was an elaborate affair, with all the trappings, and he was horrified. He said weddings were a female conspiracy for making men look ridiculous, and he'd never let it happen to him. With anyone else you could say, "You're always ridiculous," or some such backchat. But not with Steven. Even then he was always on top.' He checked himself guiltily. 'Look, I've probably said more than I should—'

'Nonsense. What harm can it do?' she asked brightly.

'Your friend's coming back. I'd better go now.'

'Don't forget these.' She pushed the cufflinks towards him.

'If you're sure—thanks.'

David, who'd been nearing the table, watched him depart, and turned a quizzical look on Jennifer. 'Have you given a set of those cufflinks to every man in London, or just the ones I see you with?' he asked. 'Jennifer? Jennifer?'

'I'm sorry,' she said hastily, returning to reality.

'Well?'

'I beg your pardon?'

'Have you come to any conclusion?'

'Yes,' she said, her eyes alight. 'I've decided it's time I played a little game of my own.'

CHAPTER SIX

JENNIFER'S call to Steven was put through without delay.

'Jennifer,' he said cheerfully. 'What a nice surprise!'

'Shouldn't you be calling me darling?'

'No, there's nobody listening.'

She laughed. '*Touché.* How about dinner at the Ritz? My treat.'

'Fine. You observe that I'm admirably free from hang-ups about letting the woman pay. I'll even let you collect me and take me home afterwards.'

'Tomorrow night?'

'Great.'

'Steven, I have to admit I have an ulterior motive.'

'I knew you wouldn't disappoint me,' he said appreciatively.

'Can you help me out over a man called Martson? He's bad news, but I'd like to know just how bad.'

'He's a predator. He does all he can to weaken a company, then buys it on the cheap. But I know a few things that can be used against him. I'll have something for you by tomorrow.'

'I'm really grateful to you for taking the trouble,' she said meekly.

But she'd overdone it, because Steven immediately said, 'Jennifer, when you adopt that reasonable tone my antennae vibrate with danger. You're up to something.'

'Who, *me*?'

He laughed. 'I'll see you.'

Jennifer was delighted with the success of her little

stratagem. She would let Steven knock himself out finding the information she wanted, and then she would reveal that it had all been for David's benefit. That would teach him to be so sure of his buses.

She was curious to know how his self-confidence would stand up to the discovery that she'd played him at his own game. And she would enjoy teasing him about it. That was Steven's trouble. He hadn't been teased enough.

She left work early next day, so that she could spend a long time grooming herself for the evening ahead. She had a new black dress, shot through with silver glitter, and she didn't even try to pretend that it wasn't for Steven's benefit.

The traffic was lighter than she'd expected, and she reached his house twenty minutes early. It was a large, modern building in an expensive, tree-lined avenue.

Maud let her in. She too was dressed for an evening out, in a scarlet silk creation that outlined her slender figure.

'Steven will be down directly,' she said. 'You won't mind if I have to leave you alone for a moment?'

'I can see you're getting ready for a date,' Jennifer said, studying the girl's beauty with a smile. 'He must be really special.'

To her surprise Maud blushed. It wasn't a delicate model's blush, but a fierce tide that went up to the roots of her hair and clashed with her dress. Jennifer liked Maud anyway, but she liked her even more for this chink in her flawless armour.

'Yes, he is,' Maud mumbled. 'Very special. Excuse me, I've got to go.'

From overhead came the sound of a door opening, and

feet coming downstairs. Jennifer heard Steven say, 'Maud, have you any idea where—?'

She turned quickly. Steven was standing halfway up the stairs, wearing trousers but no shirt. He halted abruptly when he saw her and she had a long moment to drink in the sight of his broad chest and muscular shoulders. Normally his sharp, well-cut suits disguised the power of his frame. Now, for the first time, she realised how magnificently he was built.

The world seemed to stop. Everything about Steven was vivid, from his heavy shoulders to the silky dark hair that covered his chest and swirled in a perfectly balanced pattern down to his waist, disappearing into his belt.

She'd tried to imagine him without clothes, but her thoughts hadn't come up with anything as splendid as this. Images chased each other, pell mell, through her brain. Mike had said, 'They were all lining up for him. Can't think why…'

But I know why, was the thought she couldn't stifle. *Lucky for me I've been warned. Another woman might have made a fool of herself over him.*

Steven's eyes showed that he too had been taken aback. They moved over her beauty with a look of appreciation, and he drew in a slow breath.

'I didn't know you were here,' he said at last.

'I'm a bit early. The traffic was light.' She had no idea what she was saying.

'I'll be with you in a minute.' He sounded vague.

Maud's eyes went from one to the other, while her lips twitched. But neither of them noticed her.

The scream of the doorbell broke the spell. Maud snatched up her wrap, muttered, 'Night, you two,' and hurried out.

As she opened the front door Jennifer caught a glimpse of the man standing there, and the joyful look on his face as he pulled Maud into his arms. Then the door shut them out.

Steven grinned at Jennifer's expression. 'That's how I felt, too,' he said. 'I'll be with you in a moment.'

He was back five minutes later in a snowy evening shirt whose elegant ruffles contrasted starkly with the harsh masculinity of his face. He looked ridiculously handsome.

And don't you just know it! she thought. *In fact, you're counting on it. Like buses, huh? What a shock you're going to get!*

He behaved beautifully, deferring to her at the car door, and not even trying to edge her out of the driving seat. Not until Jennifer was into the flow of the traffic did he drop his bombshell.

'I've changed my mind about the Ritz. I'd rather go to a nightclub.'

'But I've booked a table at the Ritz.'

'I'm afraid I took the liberty of cancelling that and booking us in at the Orchid Club.'

'Well, I suppose I might have known you'd do something outrageous and arrogant like that,' she said wryly.

'I suppose you might. Turn left up here.'

'If it's a club, won't it be members only?'

'I am a member. I'll be paying the bill too. In fact, I've taken over the whole evening. I do hope you don't mind.'

'You don't care if I mind or not. Steven, I don't want to go to a nightclub. It's too—' She nearly said intimate, but stopped herself. 'It's just not what I had in mind.'

'Don't be ungrateful after all the trouble I've taken to find out about Martson for you.'

'Really? Have you come up with much?'

'Enough to be interesting. Now can we go to the Orchid Club?'

'To the ends of the earth,' she said gaily.

'Be careful what you say. I may hold you to it.'

Jennifer laughed. Suddenly she felt wonderful. It was a glorious night. But that, of course, was because she was looking forward to taking the wind out of his sails.

When she saw the Orchid Club she knew Steven had out-manoeuvred her, which was impressive for a man who didn't even know the game they were playing. The nightclub was very exclusive, discreet and intimate. The doorman greeted Steven as a regular customer and gave Jennifer a swift, appraising glance that suggested she was the latest in a long line. This wasn't how things had been meant to go. But her moment would come.

Their table was in a dark corner, lit by one small lamp. Steven handed her to her seat and ordered wine, which the waiter brought.

'Well, here we are,' he said when he'd given their order.

'Yes, but—here.' She indicated their surroundings. 'This was supposed to be my treat.'

'What does it matter? I'm flattered by your eagerness to see me.'

'Don't kid yourself. It's your advice I'm eager for.'

'About Martson? He's an unpleasant character, but he's not in Nortons' league.'

'There are—reasons—why he's very important to me.'

He regarded her quizzically. It was so clear that he thought she'd made an excuse to see him that Jennifer began to feel a tingle of anticipation. She was going to enjoy this evening.

'Where's David tonight?' he asked suddenly.

Caught off guard, she stammered, 'I—I don't know.'

'Does he know where you are? Never mind. If he doesn't, he ought to. If I was in love with a woman I'd lock her up before I'd let her play the kind of game you're playing with me.'

'Maybe she wouldn't agree to be locked up.'

His answer was to take her hand and drop his head until his lips brushed the palm. 'Maybe I could make her want to agree,' he whispered.

She couldn't reply, although she knew Steven must be able to feel her pulses racing. He raised his eyes, giving her a look that devastated her.

'You don't know what game I'm playing with you,' she said at last.

'I know you're using me to make him jealous, and for the good of your firm. Are you saying there's more?'

She smiled mysteriously. 'There could be.'

'What a little devil you are! All right, I'll go for it. A touch of the devil makes a woman perfect. Are there any rules?'

'You'll find them out by trial and error.'

'And you?'

'I make them up as I go along.'

He released her hand and raised his glass to her, his eyes full of admiration. He thought he was treading a well-worn path, Jennifer mused. First the woman teased him, then she fell into his arms: it was so familiar to him. But tonight he was in for a shock.

'Why are your eyes gleaming in that delicious way?' he asked.

'Wait and see.'

'All right, Jennifer. It's your game. But I distrust you tonight.'

'I distrust you all the time,' she riposted. 'You must admit, it gives a certain piquancy to our dealings.'

'True. You never bore me for an instant. How are you going to surprise me?'

'If I told you that, it wouldn't be a surprise. Leave it for now. Tell me, is our little masquerade going well?'

'People think we're mad about each other.'

'No, I meant the market,' she said, with a little air of surprise. 'After all, that's what really matters.'

He grinned his admiration of this touch. 'Certainly it is. Well, Charteris's value has leapt up now the market's expecting us to tie up with you.'

'"Tie up with us",' Jennifer said thoughtfully. 'As in "eat us alive"?'

He laughed. 'I don't think I could put one across on you.'

'Oh, yes, you do. You also think you've got me fooled.'

He poured some wine into her glass, and wasn't looking at her as he said, 'Am I trying to do that, Jennifer?'

'Is there any woman you don't try to fool?'

'Is there any woman who doesn't want to be fooled?'

'Oh, yes. Right here. I value plain dealing.'

'Then you're different from all other women in creation.'

She leaned a little closer, over the table. 'I don't respond to flattery,' she said, in a voice so soft that only he could hear it.

He too leaned forward, until their hair was almost touching. 'Then I'll tell you, in plain, unvarnished words, that you're the most sensationally sexy woman I've ever known. I always study your clothes to guess how easy they'd be to remove. I know you don't plan to let me remove them—not yet anyway—but I can't help it. It's instinctive. When we talk I can't keep my mind on the words because I'm thinking how badly I want to see you naked, and to be naked with you, and all the things I want us to do together.'

The pleasure was rising in her at the delightful pictures he conjured up. But she refused to yield to it. Tonight, she was going to stay in control.

'Do you think you'll manage it?' she asked.

'Do *you* think I will?'

'Never.'

'Would you care to make a little bet on that?'

'The last time we made a bet you cheated,' she reminded him.

'And I'll cheat again if it'll get you into my bed. Why waste time with honest methods when cheating produces results?'

'But you're an honest man in business.'

'Perhaps business isn't so important.'

'Shame on you, Steven. Nothing is more important than business.'

Instead of answering he reached out a finger and drew it lightly down her cheek, then along the outline of her lips. The effect was so delightful that she took a long, quivering breath. 'You don't really believe that,' he murmured.

'No, but you do.'

'We could make something more important—if we wanted to.'

'Something?'

'Us.'

He was falling for it, she thought with an inner smile. Or rather, he thought *she* was falling for his sweet-talking ways.

'What do you say to that?' he asked.

'I say the waiter is standing just behind you,' she replied primly.

He grimaced before drawing back to sit watching her while the waiter served them. His eyes glinted in the dim light, reminding her of things she'd have been wiser to forget, or never to have known.

When they were alone again Steven regarded her quizzically, to see if she would take up the subject, but she refused to do so. Let him wonder!

'How are the little ones?' he asked, starting on his meal.

'We've passed two milestones,' Jennifer said, getting onto her favourite subject. 'They've all opened their eyes, and this morning the last one left the basket. That's the boy. He seems to be a late developer.''

'That's the one you named after me, isn't it?'

'I'm afraid so. Never mind. He'll catch up. The one who opened her eyes first is really advanced. She scampers everywhere, while the others just sit in the middle of the carpet and squeak. They're so sweet and tiny…'

He grinned at the sight of her face as she chattered on, her eyes alight with love for her tiny charges. That was a very special look, he realised. It was open, defenceless, vulnerable. Was there any human being she trusted enough to look like that? he wondered. Certainly not himself. David? He would have given a lot to know the answer to that question.

Jennifer had finished talking about the cats and remembered something else. 'Did I really see who I thought I saw collect Maud tonight?' she asked. 'Trevor?'

'You didn't imagine it. Those two are besotted with each other. Hasn't he said anything?'

'Not a word. Mind you, I haven't seen him except at

work, and recently he's been leaving the office early—
oh, of course!'

'No prizes for guessing whom he's been hurrying off
to meet,' Steven said, grinning. 'What about his mood?
There's no getting any sense out of Maud.'

'Well, he's seemed a bit preoccupied, but then he always has a lot on his mind.'

'It's my sister who's on his mind at the moment. Not
that he's got much to worry about. She isn't exactly
playing hard to get.'

'How long have you known?'

'Since the first evening. She told me on the way home
that she was going to marry him.'

'Love at first sight,' Jennifer mused. 'I never really
believed in it before. I guess Trevor's found what he
needs at last.'

'And what's that?'

'When our mother died,' Jennifer said after a slight
hesitation, 'we clung together. He was sixteen and I was
twelve, but I comforted him more than the other way
around. We were so close in those days. It was like we
were always holding each other's hands.

'But then he started to hang around with a gang, and
I guess he was too proud to hold my hand any more. So
he let go and never came back. But it was too soon. He
couldn't cope. I think he's been looking for someone to
comfort him ever since.'

'Surely Barney was there for you?'

'Not in that way. He loved us, but he was always
busy.'

'And what about you?' Steven asked, looking at her
curiously. 'Whose hand did you hold?'

'Nobody's, I guess.' Something caught in her throat
as the memory came back to her of long, lonely nights,

weeping for her mother, her father, or Trevor, or her grandfather—or anyone.

'Jennifer?' Steven said gently, studying her face with sudden concentration.

She came back to the present, adjusting a bright smile on her face. She didn't know that the smile was wonky and unconvincing, but she felt Steven take hold of her hand and give it a comforting squeeze. For a moment they sat in silence. There was nothing to say, but his hand was warm.

'You realise what you've just told me, don't you?' he asked gently. 'The secret of David Conner's attraction. You perceive him as solid and reliable.'

'He's always there when I need him—'

'Not now, he isn't. That's why you're clinging onto the thought of him like grim death.'

'I seem to be clinging to you,' she said awkwardly, releasing her hand.

'The fact is, you're afraid of being abandoned again. You're not really in love with him at all.'

'Why shouldn't I want to be safe?' she demanded.

'I could give you a thousand reasons, but I'll settle for this one. You want marriage, and the illusion of safety it brings. This is the real Jennifer Norton. Underneath that smart, sophisticated exterior is a little girl looking for a hand to hold in the dark.

'Well, I'm not a marrying man, but I'm better for you than Conner is because we understand each other. Jennifer, believe me, there's more safety in being with someone who thinks and feels as you do—even if only for a day—than in all the wedding rings in the world.'

She didn't know how to answer. Her heart was beating strongly, not with the sweet sexual excitement he could evoke in her so easily, but with a kind of alarm as he came so dangerously near to her innermost sanctum.

The next moment he invaded her secret world even further with the blunt words, 'Don't force the poor sap to marry you, Jennifer. You'll regret it all your life.'

'That's nonsense,' she said, speaking roughly to cover her turmoil. 'I couldn't force David to marry me.'

'I think you could, and I'll stop it if I can.'

'And dump me afterwards,' she challenged.

'Afterwards we'll toss our caps over the windmill. I don't think you've ever done that, and it's time you did. Maybe I wouldn't leave you. Maybe you'd leave me, and I'd come chasing after you.'

'I don't think so,' she said with a touch of wistfulness.

'Don't underestimate yourself. And forget Conner. He doesn't love you. Or if he does, it means his idea of love is as narrow as yours.'

'Steven, let's drop this,' she said in a warning voice. 'I mean it.'

'All right,' he said after a moment. 'But I'll just say this. Somehow you've got to sort out your demons, but Little Lord Fauntleroy isn't the answer.'

She choked with unwilling laughter. 'Don't call David that.'

'But you recognise him from the description?'

'You're impossible.' She was still laughing, annoyed with him for getting in under her guard with an irresistible joke. David didn't make jokes, she realised.

'What is your face revealing?' he asked, leaning towards her. 'I can't see in this light.'

'Good. The less you know about me, the better.'

'Don't tell me you're nervous? Of me?'

'No,' she said, too quickly. 'Not of you or any man.'

He said nothing, only watched her for a moment. He

was thinking how entrancing she looked when the colour came up in her cheeks, making her features even more vivid. Was she like that at the moment of true passion? he wondered. And how long would it be before he knew?

But he reined himself in. His pursuit of Jennifer had become an absorbing game, all the more fascinating because his quarry knew how to dodge and feint, how to lead him on, to draw back and send him after false trails. And—it amazed him to realise this—there was no certainty of success. He'd never yet wanted a woman that he wasn't sure of getting, and the novelty intrigued him.

'I'm glad you told me about your parents,' he said. 'It helps me see you more clearly. I'd thought of you as having an easy life, going into your grandfather's firm because it was fun.'

'I don't find it fun. I'd rather have worked with animals, but how could I tell Barney that?'

'Easily. If he really loved you he'd be glad for you to follow your own dream. He does love you, doesn't he?'

'Of course.'

'But only if you do what he wants?'

'That's not fair.'

'But do you believe it?'

'Stop trying to confuse me,' she said with a touch of desperation.

'All right,' he said quietly after a moment. 'I'm sorry.'

'Hasn't your work been fun for you?' she asked, determined to get him onto another track.

'Parts of it. Recently. Not at first.'

'I wish you'd tell me.'

He hesitated uneasily, and she guessed he didn't find it easy to confide in people, perhaps because he trusted nobody, except maybe Maud. She knew that if she could overcome this barrier she would be a step closer to the heart of the man.

At last he said, 'In a strange way, you remind me of my mother. She had a very hard life, but she never let it get her down. You were like that, going to the banquet on my arm, looking the world in the eye, not letting on how unhappy you were.

'There's nobody I've ever admired more than my mother. She faced all her misfortunes with courage, and humour. I just wish she'd lived long enough to see me make it. I'd have liked to give her some of the good things of life.'

'What about your father?'

'Died when I was fourteen. Mum was actually carrying Maud at the time. I'm the only father Maud's ever known.'

'Tell me more about your mother,' Jennifer begged.

'She was great. Not that I told her that at the time. After Dad died I became the man of the family. Mum still saw me as a kid. We had a few fights about that. I got a job delivering papers for the corner shop. When I found another one, stacking shelves in a supermarket on weekends, she had to admit I was a man.'

'She let you do two jobs? At fourteen?'

'I didn't ask her. I just did what I had to.'

'What about your education?'

'I managed. I left school early, got myself a market stall selling anything I could pick up cheap. When I'd made a small profit I got another stall.'

'How did you get from market stalls to Charteris?' Jennifer asked, genuinely fascinated.

'I took commercial courses at night school, and I moved into little shops that were near the end of their lease. In the end I owned three shops, but I wanted to play in the big league, so I sold up and got a job with Charteris. I ploughed the profit from the shops into Charteris shares, and in ten years I was running the firm. They didn't want to appoint me. They saw me as a jumped-up barrow boy—which I am. But there was nobody else who could drag them up to date.'

The completeness of his assurance almost took the words beyond arrogance. This man knew he was born to rule, and there was no need for further discussion.

'Over the years,' he went on, 'I've taken share options, bought more stock in Charteris whenever I could.'

'So now you have a power base.'

'Right. And money. Which matters. I've seen how terrifying the lack of money can be, how it eats you up and controls the whole of your life. I've lain awake, wondering if I could get this payment in in time to meet that bill, and, if not, how could I talk my way out of it? I've had people who thought they could put one over on me, because they saw me as just a kid. And I had to teach them the hard way that they were wrong.'

'The hard way?'

'There's no other way that works,' he said simply. 'If you're retaliating, you must do it so powerfully that the enemy won't challenge you again.'

He spoke in a matter-of-fact way that made Jennifer give a little shiver.

'I'm glad I haven't made an enemy of you,' she said.

He looked at her strangely. 'I'm glad you haven't, too,' he said.

CHAPTER SEVEN

SHE let him drive on the home journey, content to sit beside him in a pleasant glow.

'This will give me a chance to visit Paws and family,' he said. 'I'm curious to see how far they've come on.'

Jennifer's first act on getting home was to rush to the basket, but there was nobody at home.

'There's one here,' Steven called, scooping up a kitten from behind the sofa, 'and one over there.'

'Since they got out of the box I never know where I'm going to find them,' she said, laughing.

Paws appeared from the kitchen and joined in the hunt, and soon everyone was back where they belonged. Steven made warm milk for the cats and coffee for them. Jennifer was beginning to feel like a cat herself, a contented cat, stretching and luxuriating in the feeling that all was right with the world.

'By the way,' Steven said, 'we forgot something.'

'Did we?'

'Martson. You wanted to pick my brains about him, and we haven't discussed him at all.'

With a shock she remembered that this whole evening had been about putting Steven Leary in his place. It had been conceived as a light-hearted prank, but now it seemed silly and schoolgirlish. Tonight she'd learned things about him that intrigued her, and she'd let him see into her own secret heart where intruders weren't allowed. Now she no longer wanted to laugh at him, teach him a lesson, or do anything except kiss him.

'Do you want to talk about it now?' he asked.

'No—no, another time. It's not important,' she stammered, hardly knowing what she said.

'No,' he agreed, taking her into his arms. 'It's not important.'

She was beginning to be afraid of Steven's kisses. She wanted them too much. He was like an addiction, bad and dangerous for her, but impossible to resist. She'd push him away next time, but tonight she must kiss him back eagerly, burningly—just once more.

But as with all addictions there was no such thing as 'just once more'. For him too. One kiss became another and another, and suddenly he was raining kisses all over her face and neck.

'I want you,' he murmured, 'and I want you to want me.'

'You know that I—I don't know—Steven—'

Words dissolved into nothing as she began kissing him back urgently. Her head was full of pictures of Steven as she'd seen him at the start of the evening, stripped to the waist, broad-shouldered and muscular, the hair of his torso vanishing into his belt. The need to touch him had been growing in her from that moment until it was almost unbearable.

She saw his eyes, heavy with passion, gazing down on her with a strange, bewildered look, as if he found it hard to believe what was happening. 'You're always more beautiful than I remember,' he said thickly.

His hands moved on the flimsy dress. She knew that soon nothing would stop them. She was hurtling headlong towards something she desired with every fibre of her being, and yet...

The words that came out of her mouth were the last she'd expected to utter.

'Steven—Steven wait—'

She could sense the effort it cost him to leash himself back. 'What is it, Jennifer? What's wrong?' His voice was ragged with strain.

'I don't know—suddenly everything's going too fast—I'm not ready for this—'

She braced herself for his rage at being thwarted, but it didn't come. His face was very pale but he had himself under control. He even managed a kind of joke.

'Jennifer, your sense of timing is something wonderful. Do you think I can stop now?'

'I think you can do anything you set your mind to,' she said shakily.

'Oh, you clever, clever woman,' he breathed. 'Damn you for knowing the right thing to say!'

He released her slowly, painfully. As soon as she drew back from him he turned away, running his hands through his hair.

'I'm sorry,' he said distractedly.

He couldn't have said anything that would have surprised her more. Steven Leary had apologised. It was as if the stars had stopped in their tracks.

'It's my fault,' she said shakily, 'for not knowing my own mind.'

'Let's not argue about whose fault it is. I don't think I could stand that at this moment.' He gave an edgy laugh. 'It's not like me to misread things so badly.'

'You didn't,' she said haltingly. 'It was me—I just freaked out. I don't know why.'

'I'll go now if you want.'

'Yes, maybe you should.'

She longed to ask him to stay, but knew she mustn't. In another moment he would be out of the door and their relationship would be over, for she must never, never see him like this again.

The scream of the doorbell startled them both. They seemed to wake and look around them, wondering what had brought them here. Jennifer pulled herself together and opened her front door. A man and woman, both in their forties, stood on the step, with a girl of about ten.

'We're sorry to trouble you at this hour,' the woman said. 'We've been calling all evening, but there was nobody in. Brenda should have been in bed ages ago, but we didn't have the heart to make her go home, not if there was a chance of getting Snowy back.'

'Snowy?' Jennifer asked with a sinking heart.

'Because she's got snowy white paws, though the rest of her's black,' the little girl said. Then a joyous smile broke over her face, and she shrieked, *'Snowy!'*

She darted into the house to envelop Paws, who'd come dashing towards her. With a rueful smile Jennifer beckoned the parents in. Steven closed the door and stood quietly watching.

There were rapid introductions. Mr and Mrs Cranmer were armed with family photographs, showing Paws/ Snowy in the little girl's arms. There was no doubt that these were the cat's rightful owners. Young Brenda had already discovered the kittens and was cuddling them blissfully.

'We live four roads away,' Mrs Cranmer said. 'One of our neighbours said someone in this road had taken in a black cat with white paws, but she wasn't sure who. We've been knocking on doors round here, and someone said it was you. We were so worried when she disappeared so near her time. We had visions of her giving birth in a gutter with nobody to look after her. Thank goodness she was safe with you.'

'You must let us refund anything you spent on a vet,' Mr Cranmer insisted.

'The vet only arrived when the job was done,' Jennifer said. 'Steven did it all himself.'

Over coffee and cocoa they told the story of that night. There was much laughter, but Steven, watching closely, saw that Jennifer's smiles were a little forced. He met her eyes, his own full of warmth and understanding.

When it was time for the visitors to go Snowy jumped into Jennifer's lap and rubbed her head against her, purring noisily.

'She's saying thank you,' Brenda said wisely. 'She loves you.'

'I love her,' Jennifer said huskily. 'And I'm so happy that she's found her family again.'

'But you'll be on your own,' Brenda said. 'Would you like one of her kittens?' She held out the boy, whose markings were almost identical to Snowy's. 'I'll bring him round when he's old enough to leave his mother,' she offered.

Reluctantly Jennifer shook her head.

'I'd love to,' she said. 'But it wouldn't be kind to leave him alone in this house while I'm out all day. It was different with P— with Snowy. For her, even being left alone here was better than the street. But this little fellow has other options.'

'Don't you want him?' Brenda asked.

'Yes, I want him very much, but—' Her voice broke.

'We understand,' Mrs Cranmer said gently.

Steven watched as she closed the door after the family, and saw the way her shoulders sagged. She kept her back to him, then went into the kitchen and out of sight.

Steven called himself a taxi. While he dialled, he kept

his attention on the kitchen, and heard the sound of her blowing her nose.

'The taxi will be here in two minutes,' he said as she returned.

'Fine,' she said, smiling brightly, but he knew her brightness would fade the moment he'd gone. She would be really alone then, without the cats that had needed her, without David, without himself, without anyone. The thought of the loneliness she wouldn't acknowledge hurt him.

The words came out of their own accord. 'Spend tomorrow with me, Jennifer.'

'I—I've got meetings all day—' she stammered.

'Cancel them. Take the day off. Come with me to the seaside.'

'The seaside?' she echoed, not sure she'd heard him right.

'I want to take you to Huntley and show you where I grew up. Let's go mad.'

'Oh, yes, let's,' she said, suddenly as thrilled as a child.

'I'll collect you here at eight, tomorrow morning. Don't be late. Goodnight.'

When he'd gone Jennifer paced the floor restlessly, trying to organise her thoughts. She wanted Steven so much that she couldn't think straight, yet she'd refused to yield to her own desires.

Why had she panicked? Perhaps because her longing for Steven threatened to become stronger than she was, and disrupt the orderly life she'd promised herself long ago, when she'd been a lonely, abandoned child.

She'd only half expected him to be there next morning, but at five minutes to eight he was knocking on her door. She opened to find a man she barely recognised.

Steven Leary, in a check shirt and jeans? Steven Leary, without a tie? And smiling like a kid looking forward to a treat?

His look mirrored her own. Fawn trousers and a buttercup yellow shirt was an ensemble she would never have worn to work. Neither would she have knotted the rust silk scarf about her neck, or shouldered the gaily decorated canvas bag.

'Aren't you ready yet?' he demanded.

'Cheeky so-and-so! I need ten minutes.'

The words were mundane, but beneath them lay something else: question and answer. How is he/she looking at me now? What has changed between us?

But for the moment, at any rate, they could cover the tension with an air of normality.

'You're dressed just right for a day by the sea,' he said when she was ready.

'Well, I hope it's a proper seaside,' she told him severely. 'With a sandy beach, and a cove, with a whelk stall and a man selling ice creams.'

'I'm afraid the beach is shingle,' he said. 'But there was a cove and a man selling ice creams. I'm sure they won't have changed.'

'When I was a child our parents used to take Trevor and me to the seaside,' Jennifer said as Steven headed his car out onto the road. 'Those trips still have a golden glow in my mind. The sun was always shining, the ice creams were always delicious, and Trevor and I were always squabbling about whose sandcastle was the biggest.'

'I'll bet you won.'

'Not always. But he used to cheat.'

'By the way, speaking of Trevor, Maud didn't come

home last night—not for the first time. I think we should start preparing for the wedding.'

'You're not serious?'

'You don't know my little sister when she's made up her mind. She's awesome.'

Jennifer was about to argue when she recalled Trevor's face as he'd taken Maud into his arms. It had borne a look of total, humble adoration.

'You say she decided on the first evening,' she said, a little troubled. 'Then can she really love him?'

'Why else should she want to marry him?'

'Well—there comes a time in the life of every model…' Jennifer paused delicately.

'She's not marrying him for financial security, if that's what you think.' Steven kindly helped her out. 'She's got plenty of money of her own, I promise you. Why? Don't you believe in love at first sight?'

'Do you?' she asked, startled.

'I believe in something at first sight. As for love—' He shrugged. 'It's obvious what the word means to Maud, but for me—' He checked himself. 'I guess everyone sets their own meaning.'

'I don't think you do know how Maud defines it,' Jennifer said thoughtfully. 'Obviously she sees something in Trevor that's hidden from us. Maybe that instinctive insight is love. And trusting the other person enough to let them see the truth about you. If they've found it, I envy them.'

'But you've found it,' he pointed out. 'You and David.'

'David and I love each other, but you know it's not simple and untroubled, the way it seems to be with Trevor and Maud.'

'Perhaps if it's troubled, it isn't love at all,' he suggested mildly.

'I'm not giving up on it just because we have a few problems. Most couples do. We'll work it out. Is it very far to Huntley?'

'Sixty miles,' he said, accepting her change of subject without demur. 'It's just a little place, or it was when I last saw it. It wasn't a popular resort for family holidays because of the pebble beach, so it stayed quiet and uncommercial, and a lot of elderly people used to retire there. When I was a kid I thought it was too sleepy, but I'm getting to the age when I appreciate the peace.'

'Into the sear and yellow,' she said appreciatively, regarding his powerful body. 'Did you remember to bring your Zimmer frame?'

'Nope. I'm planning to lean on you.'

She watched his hands on the wheel, controlling the heavy vehicle without effort. They were shapely hands, muscular and beautiful, and last night they had held her with passion, demanding yet also giving, knowing just where and how to touch her. And yet she'd sent him away. Was she mad?

Before long she could taste the salty tang in the air, and knew they were near the sea.

'There it is!' she cried, as she'd done as a child. 'I just glimpsed it between those trees.'

The water was dazzling in the sunlight, and she knew a thrill of the old excitement. Soon the sea appeared again, this time for longer, and at last they were on the coast road, with the shore beside them all the way.

'There was a whelk stall just past here,' Steven remembered. 'No sign of that any more.'

But they found a good seafood restaurant and sat by the window enjoying the view.

'There are more people here than I recall,' he said. 'Huntley must have prospered. Good for Dan Markham.'

'Who's Dan Markham?'

'He owned the corner shop and gave me my first job, delivering papers. I still shudder when I think of getting up at six on those winter mornings. But he always gave me a hot drink before I went out with the papers, and another one when I got back. He was a great old boy.'

Jennifer had never heard him speak so warmly of anyone before. 'Tell me more about him,' she said, glad to keep him in this mood.

'He looked like Santa Claus, with a bushy white beard and a twinkle in his eye. And he was generous to the point of foolhardiness. He paid me more than the going rate, and he increased that when my mother died.'

'A rotten businessman,' Jennifer observed with a smile.

'Terrible,' Steven agreed. 'He'd give customers credit, and then write it off because they were nice people.'

'Shocking! I hope you lectured him about his inefficiency.'

'I did. I can hear myself now, fourteen years old and saying, "You've cut your profit margins to ribbons, Mr Markham." And he stared at me blankly, and said, "I don't know about profit margins, lad. I just buy and sell things." While his wife was alive she'd done the books. After a while I took them over. That was when I discovered how much my own mother had benefited from his charity.'

He finished drily, and for a moment his eyes were dark, as though even now the memory had power to hurt.

'I'll bet you paid him back every penny,' Jennifer said.

He gave her a sudden, startled look. 'Am I that transparent?'

'Well, I think I'm beginning to know you a little.'

'Yes, I guess you are. I calculated what we owed him, and I refused to take another penny in wages until I'd worked it off. He and I had some terrible rows about it, but I won.'

'Of course,' Jennifer murmured.

'I paid him back and I tried to teach him good business practice. But I never managed it. The place went downhill for years, and he simply couldn't understand why.'

Jennifer regarded him with fascination. Steven Leary did have a heart. Not the melting, sentimental kind, but a rough, powerful organ that behaved awkwardly but was honest and good, even kind. It was a heart she increasingly wanted to know about. Even, perhaps, to possess.

'Did he lose the shop in the end?' she asked.

'Nearly. Luckily someone stepped in and hauled him out of the mire.'

'No prizes for guessing who.'

After a moment he gave a grin with a touch of sheepishness. 'Yes, all right. It was me. I happened to be passing near Huntley a few years ago and dropped in to see him. He was about to be forced out, and I'm a man who likes to pay my debts, so I made him a loan.'

'Did he ever manage to repay you?'

Laughing, he shook his head. 'I had to write it off,' he admitted. 'The paperwork was just too much trouble.'

'Don't make excuses. You were fond of him. Sheer human weakness.'

'I don't have any human weaknesses,' he defended himself. 'Not the amiable kind, anyway.'

'Paws could say a thing or two about that.'

'Helping Paws that night was sheer practical efficiency to stop you having hysterics.'

'You're a fraud. Underneath that steel exterior—'

'Beats a steely heart,' he interrupted. 'Don't go crediting me with melting qualities. I owed that old man. End of story.'

'If you say so.'

When they resumed their journey the road turned inland for a spell, then abruptly back to the coast.

'These apartment blocks are new,' Steven observed. 'Ugly great things! Good grief!'

Jennifer followed his gaze to the horizon, where a huge ferris wheel had come into view between the apartment blocks. Noisy music floated in their direction, and bright lights flickered.

'That monstrosity is new,' Steven groaned. 'It looks like the developers have moved in.'

Closer to Huntley it became clear just how much the developers had taken over. Modern buildings were everywhere, garishly lit shops lined the promenade, and the little town was crowded with people.

'It's not the place I knew any more,' Steven said heavily. 'But why has everyone suddenly come here?'

They had one answer a few minutes later, in a huge casino that overlooked the sea.

'It pulls them in from miles around,' the doorman confided. 'Open twenty-four hours a day. Always something going on. The kids love it.'

'I'll bet they do,' Steven said in horror.

'Good investment,' Jennifer reminded him.

'Not in my backyard,' he growled without irony. 'I just hope it did old Dan some good.'

He set off in search of the corner shop, and to

Jennifer's relief they saw a bright, cheerful shop bearing the name 'Markham's Newsagent'.

'He made a success of it finally,' Steven said with relief.

'Thanks to you.'

'Let's go and give him a shock,' he said, seizing her hand and almost running inside.

A sleek young man was in attendance behind the counter. 'What can I do for you, sir?' he asked, smiling blandly.

'Is Dan Markham around?' Steven asked.

'Dan—? Oh, you mean old Mr Markham. I think he went to Canada.'

'He's on vacation in Canada?' Steven echoed in dismay.

'No, he sold up.'

'Sold up? But the name—'

'Oh, yes, it's still called Markham's because that's what people are used to, but actually the shop's owned by a chain now. They bought it from Dan Markham.'

'You mean they drove him out,' Steven said grimly.

'Didn't have to. He was only too eager to sell. The bloke he owed money to had just written off the whole debt—more fool him! A week later Dan sold this place. He said he was glad to take the money and run.'

'I see,' Steven said slowly. 'Yes, I see.'

He walked slowly out of the shop.

Jennifer followed him anxiously. Steven's face was pale, as though he'd received a shock, and she discovered that she could feel sorry for him. In the context of his whole life this was so trivial. And yet...

She tried to tuck her hand into his arm. He didn't throw her off, but he barely relaxed enough for her to manage it. He was walking along the street with his head down, scowling, seemingly lost in his own world of anger and dismay.

'It matters, doesn't it?' she asked sympathetically.

'Yes, it matters,' he said heavily. 'I don't know why but—hell, yes, it matters.'

His arm relaxed a little more and she was able to tuck her hand in properly. 'Let's go for a walk.'

They crossed the road and strolled down onto the beach. Some hardy bathers were bobbing about in the water, but on the whole the beach was sparsely populated. These days people came to Huntley for the gambling and the garish entertainments, and the peaceful haven that had lived in Steven's mind had vanished for ever.

They rounded a small headland and found themselves in the little cove she'd wanted. There was nobody else in sight and they were well clear of the bathers by now. Steven stopped abruptly and, seizing up a handful of pebbles, began to hurl them savagely into the water. Each one went further than the last, as though he was trying to work off his feelings.

'"More fool him!"' he echoed bitterly. 'More fool *me*!'

'Why does it matter so much?'

'A week! He must have known he was going to sell. He played me for a sucker.'

'Looks like he learned something from you after all, then.'

He scowled at her, but a moment later he put his arm around her shoulders. She slipped her own arm about his waist and they walked on, hearing the shingle crunch under their feet. Neither of them spoke for a long time, but she was content to leave it at that. Time slipped past and she realised that they'd travelled a considerable distance. The town lay behind them and they were alone on the beach, with only the waves for company.

With nobody to see, she put her arms about his neck and looked him in the face. 'Don't be hurt,' she said softly.

But he was, and it was worse for him because he wasn't used to the pain of disillusion, and didn't know how to cope. She felt a rush of tenderness for him, and was instantly disconcerted. This was what she felt for David, and it was perilously close to love. She'd promised herself not to love Steven Leary.

His next words troubled her even more. 'I'm glad you were with me when I found out.'

She heard the faint, worrying echo of other, similar words, spoken at another time, by another man. But the echo faded before she could place it.

Steven drew her close, not kissing her, but holding her as if for comfort. She hugged him back fiercely, longing to take all his troubles onto herself. How naturally his head seemed to fit on her shoulder.

'OK. I've worked off my temper now,' he said at last with a rueful sigh. 'Sorry to drag you so far. I'm acting like a jerk, aren't I?'

'No way. But can we get the bus back? I'm about walked out.'

He took her hand. 'Come on. Let's get out of Huntley all together. I don't care if I never see the place again.'

CHAPTER EIGHT

THEY got a bus back to town, found the parked car and headed out.

'Well, that wasn't the day I'd planned,' he said wryly as he drove. 'But it was instructive.'

He pulled in to an old-fashioned pub with a thatched roof and outside tables shaded by big coloured umbrellas. They ate at a table near the duck pond, tossing titbits to the quacking inhabitants.

'Look at it another way,' Jennifer said gently. 'You were fond of him, and you owed him. You paid your debts by giving him a prosperous retirement. Why shouldn't he have it his way?'

He nodded abstractedly and ate in silence for a while. At last he said, 'You're right, of course. Who was I to demand that he pickle himself in aspic for my sake? He was an old man. He must have been fed up with working by then.'

'But it's not the same, is it?'

'No, I still have this irrational feeling that he betrayed my trust—which is nonsense, I suppose.' He gave her a wry smile. 'My trouble is that I like arranging people's lives. And mostly I get away with it, which makes me worse.'

'And you're worse still when you don't get away with it?' she teased.

His smile became a broad grin. 'I'm hell on earth when I don't get my own way,' he admitted. 'I don't know why I'm making so much of it. I suppose he was

117

a benchmark in my mind: someone to trust in a wicked world.'

'Don't you trust anyone else?'

'Yes, you,' he said unexpectedly. He watched her startled face and said, amused, 'That stopped you in your tracks.'

'You couldn't have said anything that would have surprised me more.'

'I trust you completely. Despite our battles I think you're the most totally honourable person I've ever known. I think—in fact, I know—that you'd never play anyone false who trusted you.'

That Steven Leary, of all people, should pay her such a tribute left her speechless. There was a warm note in his voice that she'd never heard before, and a new look in his eyes as he took her hand gently in his. 'Jennifer—'

'Steven, please! My life is complicated, and you complicate it more.'

'Because of David?'

'Well—yes. Aren't I playing him false?'

'No. You and David are moving naturally and inevitably to the end. You're not suited, and you're both beginning to see it.' When she didn't answer he intensified his hold on her hand and asked, 'Did you call him last night, after I'd gone?'

'No,' she said quietly.

She should have called David, who was waiting anxiously to know about Martson. But she hadn't been able to force herself to do it.

'Did he call you?'

'No. Don't ask me about David, Steven.'

'I can't help it. I'm jealous. Maybe I have no right, but I'm jealous of every man who's known you in the

past, who's touched you, who's kissed you, who's—
devil take it! I can't go on like this.'

'Perhaps we should stop seeing each other?'

'Do you want to do that?' he asked quickly.

Slowly she shook her head. But the way she'd tricked
him into last night's meeting suddenly seemed terrible
after his homage to her honesty.

'Steven—there's something I should tell you—about
why I called you yesterday—'

'Hush!' He touched his lips with his fingers. 'There's
no need to tell me anything. I know you better than you
think.'

'Maybe you don't know me so well.'

'I know the important things, like the truth of your
heart. You called me for—reasons of your own, shall we
say? Some things should remain unspoken.'

He thought she'd dreamed up an excuse to seek his
company, she realised. But then, hadn't she?

She couldn't say any more. She was falling under a
spell, feeling that his heart was finally opening to her.
She'd just risked throwing that away, but she didn't dare
risk it again. It was too precious. And it was such an
innocent little deception, made in another life, when
she'd been a different person. The woman who was falling in love with Steven Leary had only been born a few
moments ago. She would bury her secret deep, where it
could never threaten them.

They spoke little for the rest of the meal. She was
content simply to sit there in the setting sun, enjoying
his company and the feeling that they were growing
closer. He was arrogant, prickly and awkward, rude
when it suited him, unreasonable, demanding and difficult. But the unexpected glimpse of his vulnerability
she'd been granted today had touched her heart. Briefly,

he'd needed her, and he hadn't been afraid to show it. From there, everything else had followed, until now she stood on the threshold of a new and wonderful future.

His barriers were coming down for her and, most remarkable of all, he seemed content to have it so. When he glanced up suddenly and smiled, there was acceptance in his eyes, and a curious puzzled look. She understood that. She felt exactly the same.

They went home slowly. Once, when they paused at traffic lights, he took her hand in his and squeezed it briefly, then drove on without a word. She felt aglow with happiness. Passion was sweet, but just as sweet was this growing closeness.

When the car stopped he said, 'I still haven't explained that Martson file to you. I left it in your house this morning. I'd better come in and tell you now.'

'Martson?' she asked in a daze. 'Oh, yes, Martson.'

She hadn't remembered. Everything but Steven now seemed so far away. As they went inside, each movement seemed heightened, the edges sharper. The sound of her key in the lock seemed enormously significant, and so did the click as he shut the door behind them and stood looking at her. It was dark by now, but her curtains were still open, letting in enough light to show her his eyes, full of a confusion that she'd never seen before. She too was confused, and could only whisper his name. The next moment she was in his arms, feeling his lips on hers.

It was a different kiss from any other he'd given her. Before she'd always felt the hint of ruthlessness, the possessiveness that fuelled his nature. This time she sensed a hunger, almost a plea, and her heart responded to it.

'You know I want you, don't you?' he murmured against her mouth.

'Yes—' she gasped. 'But—'

'Hush.' He brushed his lips across hers to silence her. '"But" is for cowards. You're no coward, Jennifer. You're strong enough to do what you want. There's only yes or no to this question.'

He was kissing her between words, teasing her with his lips, sending flickers of feeling along her ragged nerves. She tried to think, but he was purposely denying her the chance, invoking the desire that gave him the hold over her that he wanted. Jennifer clung to him, longing for the strength to break away, and longing, too, to stay in his arms for ever.

'Dump David and have an affair with me instead,' he murmured.

'An affair?'

'You don't need marriage, Jennifer, any more than I do. Let's light up the sky, go everywhere together, let the world know how we feel about each other.'

She drew back and gave him a challenging look. 'Maybe we feel different things.'

'We feel the same. It's just that I'm honest about it and you're not. We both know the score.'

'Who's keeping score?' she asked quizzically.

He laughed and nuzzled her ear. 'Do you know how badly I want to take you to bed at this moment?'

'Is that your idea of a romantic approach?'

'It's an honest approach to a woman who said she liked plain dealing.'

'Yes—yes, I do.' She couldn't remember saying it.

'You're not in love with me any more than I am with you. Are you?'

'No,' she said hazily. 'I'm not in love with you.'

'Yet we belong together: you know we do. I'll never

make you pretty speeches but I'll match you passion for passion, risk for risk. Together we'll set the sky ablaze.'

This time his kiss had a fierce, driving purpose, as though he'd cast aside doubt and was sure of victory. 'You belong to me,' he growled. 'Don't you? *Don't you?*'

She tried to answer but her senses were reeling. The word 'yes' hovered on her lips, and in a fit of madness she wanted to cry it aloud, to say that she was his and only his. Then a new life would begin for her, full of excitement and joy, full of wild and whirling passions. In another moment she would say the fatal word, and damn the consequences.

Somewhere in the background she heard the phone ring.

'Hell!' Steven muttered.

'Leave it,' she whispered. 'The answering machine is on.'

Sure enough, after a couple of rings the machine clicked in and they heard her voice suggesting the caller leave a message. Then David spoke.

'Jennifer, I've been trying to get you all day. Have you had any luck with that stuff about Martson yet? You said you had the perfect way of finding out about him, and the sooner I know the better. You know how important it is to me, darling.'

She felt Steven stiffen in her arms, and a look came over his face that almost made her cry out to see. His hands fell to his side.

'My God, but you're clever!' he said softly.

'Steven—no! It's not like that!' she said in horror.

'It's exactly like that.' He was frighteningly pale. 'You made a sucker out of me. Don't deny it. After all, it's your victory. You should be proud of it.'

'No,' she said wretchedly. 'Please—listen to me.'

'That was why you called me and asked me out, wasn't it?'

'Steven—'

'Wasn't it?'

'Yes, but—'

'And I fell for it. What a laugh that must have given you! I forgot about David, and that was stupid of me, because it's all about David, isn't it?'

'I didn't do it for David,' she cried. 'I did it for me. I wanted to take you down a peg. And, if you must know, I was going to *tell* you that the information was for him, just for the pleasure of annoying you.'

'Oh, please, you can do better than that!'

'It was stupid and I changed my mind. Today—'

'Don't mention today unless you want me to do something we'll both regret,' he said with soft savagery. 'When I think how I— *Damn you!*'

She tried to turn away from the fury in his eyes. She thought she could see pain there too, but it was hard to be certain through his anger. But she'd barely moved when he seized her shoulders and pulled her around to face him.

'Look at me,' he grated. 'Look me in the face, if you can. I thought you were an honest woman, Jennifer. I should have remembered that there's no such thing. Every woman tells a lie each time she opens her lips, and when she's kissing a man, that's when she's lying the most.'

Without warning he jerked her against him, and his mouth crushed hers in the most ruthless kiss he'd ever given her. It was compounded of desire, pain, and cold, vengeful fury. His rage alarmed her, but side by side with fear was a primitive thrill at his forcefulness. Almost in spite of herself, her lips parted and her body moved invitingly against his.

'How can any woman kiss like this, and yet it's all deception?' he growled against her mouth.

'It wasn't—' she gasped.

'Shut up! Do you think I want to hear anything you have to say?' His mouth smothered hers again, plundering, conquering, overwhelming. Fires raged through her.

'Your heart's pounding,' he mocked. 'I'll bet you even know how to fake that.'

'Steven, please—'

'Such a clever little liar! And all for what? For that mediocrity who sent you to do his dirty work. Did he think about how far you might have to go to get what he wanted? Did he care? Hell would freeze over before I'd let *my* woman run into danger for me. Or didn't you have the sense to realise you were doing something dangerous? Did you think you could jerk me around like a puppet without facing the consequences?'

Suddenly Jennifer's strength returned. Thrusting hard against him, she managed to free herself.

'I'm not afraid of you,' she flashed.

'Then you're a fool.'

'It was a silly schoolgirl trick, and I gave up the idea last night. I haven't thought about David all today. There's been no place for him in my thoughts because you—you and I—couldn't you feel that today was different—?'

'Yes, it was,' he said harshly. 'It was the day I finally saw right through you.'

She drew a sharp, painful breath. 'I want you to leave now, Steven.'

He picked up the Martson file and turned to leave.

Then he stopped, gave a short, scornful laugh, and tossed it at her.

'Take it. You worked hard enough for it,' he sneered. 'I hope Conner appreciates that. Always assuming that you tell him everything, of course.'

The door closed quietly behind him.

'Darling, you're wonderful. However did you get hold of this?' David was rustling through papers as he spoke.

'I just asked someone who's good at this kind of thing,' Jennifer said vaguely. 'As long as it's useful.'

'I'll say. There's some very sensitive material in here. Well done.' David leaned over and kissed her.

They were in his office. Jennifer had driven straight there next morning to hand over the file. She'd gone through it herself first, and knew that Steven had pulled out all the stops to do her a favour. The knowledge filled her with guilt.

Penny entered with coffee. When she'd poured it she gave Jennifer a respectful smile and withdrew.

'Penny looks a bit pale today,' Jennifer observed. 'Is she ill?'

'No, no, she's fine,' David said hurriedly. 'Actually, you're looking pale yourself.'

'I was late getting in last night.'

'That's right; I left a message on your answering machine. Did you get it all right?'

'Yes, I got it,' she said quietly.

If she was looking drawn it was because she hadn't slept a wink after Steven left. She'd tossed restlessly, and at four in the morning she'd risen, made herself some tea, and sat watching the dawn.

Normally clear-headed, she now found that she couldn't sort out her thoughts or her feelings. Anger and misery struggled for supremacy, with neither winning for very long. One moment she was furious with Steven for the things he'd said to her, the next she was full of remorse for what she'd done to him. There was an ache in her heart that wouldn't be argued away.

Yesterday she'd caught a glimpse of the man deep inside him, the man he usually tried to keep hidden. He'd opened up a little, just enough to hint at the depths of his complex personality. The night he'd tended Paws had told her that he could be kind. Now she knew that he could also be generous and sentimental, both traits he was ashamed of. And he could be more easily hurt than he wanted anyone to know.

She'd asked, 'Don't you trust anyone else?' and he'd answered, 'Yes, you,' taking her breath away. His tribute to her honesty had opened a pit at her feet. She'd tried to avoid it. It was sheer ill luck that he'd discovered her little deception—and read more into it than she had ever meant.

Again and again Jennifer went over their quarrel. Steven had been bitter, and bitterness had expressed itself as anger. Had there been an undercurrent of unhappiness, or had she imagined it? And what had lain behind his implied threat of retaliation?

She returned to her office, and for the rest of that day she became tense whenever the phone rang. But it was never Steven. Not that day, nor the next. Nor the next week.

Now that she'd been given the key, Jennifer could see the changes in Trevor. His grimness had vanished, and he smiled easily. He even laughed sometimes. He was a supremely happy man, and it had transformed him.

Even his business dealings were different, showing a

flair and adventurous spirit that had never been his before. Jennifer watched him with pleasure, but she said
nothing about the night she'd seen him with Maud. He
too never mentioned it, and she wondered if he even
knew she'd been there. He might have seen her car outside the house, but she guessed he was past noticing
anything except the woman he loved.

Then Maud herself called and invited Jennifer to
lunch, naming an Italian restaurant instead of the nou-
velle cuisine establishment Jennifer would have expected. There was a further surprise when Maud piled
her plate high, and tucked in with gusto.

'I thought models ate like birds,' Jennifer said.

Maud shook her head. 'Most of us eat like horses,'
she said. 'Besides, I'm eating for two now.'

'You mean—?'

'I'm pregnant,' Maud said triumphantly.

'But you've barely known Trevor a month.'

'We didn't waste any time,' Maud explained, patting
her stomach with a smile.

'But your career—'

'I've had that. It was very nice, but I want something
else now. I think part of me was secretly waiting for
Trevor.'

'Maud, are you actually—in love with him?'

'Of course I am.' The young woman looked shocked.
'He's gorgeous.'

'Gorgeous? Trevor?'

'He only needs someone to love and understand him.'

'He has a family.'

'But he's always felt left out by you and your grandfather.'

'I don't understand.'

'Trevor's jealous because you've always been

Barney's favourite. He adores your grandfather, tries his best to please him, but he can't break into your charmed circle.'

'He told you all this?'

'Of course not. The poor darling wouldn't know how to put it into words. But I've watched, and seen his face.'

'Are you saying this is why Trevor's been so grumpy?'

'He felt second best. But not any more.' Maud patted her stomach again. 'With us he's always going to be first.'

Jennifer smiled, truly delighted for them. 'Does he know about the baby?'

'Not yet. I'm going to surprise him tonight. I want to get married very soon. My wedding dress is really stunning, but I need to wear it quickly, before I start to put on weight.'

'Your—wedding dress?' Jennifer asked, dazed.

'I'm a very organised person,' Maud explained unnecessarily.

She knew Maud had told Trevor about the baby when he reached work humming next day. She followed him into his office.

'Can I do something for you?' he asked, with the friendliest smile he'd given her for a long time.

'You can tell me all about last night,' she said at once, adding significantly. 'I had lunch with Maud yesterday.'

Immediately a silly great grin took over his face. 'We're going to get married,' he said, and hugged her.

'I'm so glad,' she told him sincerely. 'As long as you're happy.'

'*Happy?* I didn't know what happiness was before. When I think—she's so perfect, and I'm so ordinary...'

He wasn't just saying the right thing, Jennifer realised. Trevor had never known what the right thing was. His humble words came straight from the heart.

'She's what I always wanted,' Trevor said. 'Someone who'd be mine, and there for me. After Mum died—I got lost somehow.'

'I know,' she said.

'But now I'm not alone any more,' he said simply. 'I guess you've felt alone too.'

She nodded, and smiled at him. He smiled back. They were brother and sister again.

She made some coffee and they sat talking for an hour, as they'd never talked before. Jennifer regarded her brother tenderly, delighted by the transformation in him. There had always been a nice man underneath somewhere. It had taken love to reveal that man.

This was how love ought to be, she realised: something that brought out the best in you. It should mean knowing your own heart with total certainty, not being tormented by doubt, feeling tenderness for one man, but responding helplessly to another. Love, clear and direct, making the world simple, answering all questions. Why, oh, why couldn't it be like that for her?

If anyone had told her that two nights later she would be sitting in the Savoy, celebrating her engagement to David, she would not have believed them.

CHAPTER NINE

THE day started like any other. The first sign of the earthquake to come was when David dropped into her office, looking agitated, to tell her that he'd just left Steven.

'He sent for me to say Charteris could offer me some work.'

Jennifer frowned, wondering what mischief Steven was up to. She soon found out, as David described the shocking, incredible turn the conversation had taken.

'It was a wonderful deal for me, but just when I was really fired up about it he said there was a condition.' David took a deep breath. 'I have to give you up.'

'*What?*'

'He just came right out with it. "Stay away from Jennifer Norton", he said. I thought people only acted like that in gangster movies.'

'Are you telling me,' Jennifer had said slowly, 'that Steven Leary dared—actually *dared*—?'

She could hardly speak from anger. Since the night of their quarrel her feelings towards Steven had been softer, sympathising with the pain she'd caused him. But now all that was swept away in the shock of discovering how ruthless he could be. This was Steven's revenge, a stark demonstration of power that he mustn't be allowed to get away with.

A strange look came over her face. Trevor would have recognised it and warned that it meant 'Jennifer's red mist', the herald of a wild, impulsive action that she would regret five minutes later. Her next words seemed to come out of their own accord.

'David, we have to stand up to him. Even if this hadn't happened, we'd have been thinking about the future soon.' She grasped his hands in both hers. 'Now it's time to tell everyone—and I mean *everyone*—that our marriage is going to take place, whether Steven Leary likes it or not.'

She saw the shock in his face, and for a moment almost expected him to demur. But then he said politely, 'Of course, darling. As you say, it was just a matter of time…'

Her anger carried her through the next hour, breaking the news to Trevor and Barney, calling the evening paper and inserting an announcement in time for that night's edition.

But then David departed and she was left alone, in turmoil over the effect of her hasty words. David offered the security that had always been her first need. Steven had tempted her with another life, a life of risk, where you could win or lose everything on the toss of a word. But the word had fallen against her, and it was too late. Too late.

That evening she and David dined at the Savoy, and it was everything a betrothal celebration should be, with candlelight and roses. Jennifer tried to enjoy herself, and stifle the little voice that said this was too perfect—no, not perfect, too correct—as though it were happening to a precisely written script. Tonight was what she'd longed for. And it was all wrong.

To her dismay David insisted on champagne, although white wine always gave him shattering headaches. An onlooker might have thought there was a touch of defiance in his manner, as though he were trying to convince himself of something.

'To us!' he said, raising his glass in salute.

'To us!' she responded, clinking her glass against his.

As she'd feared, the champagne gave him a migraine. His eyes were soon dark with pain and his smile became forced.

'I think we should be going,' she said gently.

He agreed gratefully, and she shepherded him out to get a taxi. It was too far to David's flat, but her own home was nearer. She could put him to bed and let him sleep off his pain.

They reached her bungalow in a few minutes, and she helped him inside. In the bedroom she pulled off his clothes and rolled him into bed. He looked up at her from the pillow, keeping a tight hold of her hand.

'You take such good care of me,' he whispered. 'Thank you, darling.'

She was swept by tenderness for him. 'I'll always take care of you,' she promised.

He smiled faintly, and closed his eyes. Jennifer released her hand and pulled open a drawer to take out a nightdress. Then she slipped away, closing the bedroom door quietly behind her.

She made up the bed in the spare room and, moving quietly, slipped into the bathroom for a shower. Perhaps the warm water pouring over her body would wash away the strange feeling of dissatisfaction on what should have been the most wonderful night of her life. She'd won the prize that had eluded her so long, and she'd shown Steven that he couldn't dictate to her. Yet she couldn't shake off her unease.

She stepped out of the shower and towelled herself vigorously. The nightdress was white and filmy, and it whispered over her head and down to the floor. In her haste she'd chosen the wrong garment. This one was designed to tease a man into removing it, not for a woman who was heading for the spare room because her lover had a headache.

Suddenly her body was alive with the desire for tender, feverish hands, touching her all over, caressing her intimately, evoking her answering passion. She closed her eyes and gradually a face formed in her dreams...

With an exclamation of dismay she opened her eyes again. How dared Steven intrude at such a moment? What business did his face have in her mind, as though the mere thought of passion evoked his image? He wasn't the man she loved, or the man she was going to marry. Yet there was no getting rid of him.

She put her head around the door for a last look at David. He'd pushed the duvet cover back and lay on the bed naked. He was beautiful, she thought, and stood watching him admiringly. But after a while she realised that her admiration was pure and dispassionate. Not a single lustful thought disturbed her.

But that was because he was ill, she thought hastily, and heard again Steven's mocking voice. 'You'd always be fighting with him for the mirror.'

She began to back out, leaving the door open in case David called out in the night.

A sharp buzz on her doorbell made her jump. Hastily she took her robe from behind the bedroom door, pulled it on over the flimsy nightie and went to answer.

Steven Leary stood on her doorstep, his eyes dark and fierce, his mouth twisted in grim, bitter lines.

'What are you doing here?' she demanded.

'Let's talk inside,' Steven said, urging her irresistibly back inside and closing the door behind him.

'We have nothing to talk about. Get out at once.'

'I'll go when I'm ready. You may not have anything to say, but I have plenty. Let's start by discussing your weird sense of humour.'

'Where you're concerned, I have no sense of humour.'

'Well, I think it's pretty funny of you to get engaged to that no-hoper and leave me to find out from the newspaper. I wonder when you were going to tell me.'

'Why should I tell you? It's none of your business.'

'You know better than that.'

He pushed past her into her front room. Jennifer had never seen him like this before. Instead of his usual immaculate appearance, his tie was missing, his shirt torn open at the throat, and his hair was awry. Strangest of all was the savage look in his eyes as they rested on her. For once, Steven wasn't in perfect control.

'I ought to shake you,' he said savagely. 'All right, we quarrelled, and maybe I said a few things—but to get back at me like *this*—!'

'Get back at you!' she echoed angrily. 'You think that's all my marriage is? A kind of revenge?'

'Don't talk to me of your marriage,' he raged. 'You have no more intention of marrying David Conner than I have. You got up this phoney engagement to pay me back. OK, I was clumsy. I should have known he'd go running to you and that you'd get so mad at me that you'd do something stupid. But this? Are you out of your mind?'

'You're wrong, Steven. This was always going to happen one day. I'm in love with David. You've known that from the first evening. And he's in love with me.'

'I know you've had some mad idea that he's the man

to solve your problems, and he's been dazzled by you like a rabbit caught in headlamps. I should have allowed for that. I didn't. I screwed up. But this is where it stops. The joke's over.'

'It's no joke.'

'Grow up, Jennifer! You can't marry him. And you don't seriously mean to. You did this to put me in my place. All right, you succeeded. I give in.'

Inexplicably, for a woman who'd just engaged herself to another man, a pulse started beating in her throat. 'And what—exactly—does ''give in'' mean?'

He turned a haggard face on her. 'Isn't it obvious?'

'Not to me.'

'I came here seeking you out, didn't I? I don't chase after women, begging favours, but I've come to ask you—plead with you—to stop this nonsense now, because otherwise—'

'Otherwise?' she asked, scarcely able to speak.

His face tensed. A man who'd found himself on the edge of a precipice might have looked as Steven did at that moment. 'Otherwise my shares will take a drop,' he finished curtly.

Jennifer stared at him, rigid with shock. 'What?' It was barely a whisper.

'Your sudden engagement can do me a lot of harm in the market.'

'I don't believe I'm hearing this,' she cried wildly. 'I don't care about the market! I'm marrying David because I love him.'

'Nonsense! You're marrying him because you lost your temper with me,' Steven retorted with devastating accuracy. 'And he's marrying you because you told him to.'

'That—isn't true,' she stammered, trying not to see

David's face in her mind, pale with shock as she arranged their marriage.

'Don't ask me to believe he proposed to you,' Steven said witheringly. 'He has too much sense of self-preservation for that. You said, ''We're not going to let him dictate to us, are we, David? We're going to get engaged just to show him.'' The poor sap never knew what hit him.'

'You have no right to say that.'

There was a burning look in his eyes that made her feel that her robe was transparent. 'I have the right to say anything that will get you out of this mess. Does he know how you come alive in my arms? Does he wonder why you're so dead in his?'

'You don't know how I am with David.'

'I know you don't burn up at his touch the way you do at mine, because no woman reacts that way to more than one man at a time. If it's there for me, it's not there for him.'

'You've changed your tune. Only a few days ago, in this very apartment, you accused me of faking it to fool you.'

'I was good 'n mad, and I had every reason. But when I calmed down I knew you couldn't pretend that much. One touch and we both go up like straw.'

'Stop it!' she cried, turning away and covering her ears.

He pulled her around to face him, giving her a little shake. 'Why? Does the truth hurt? Look me in the eyes and tell me it's not like that.'

'It's—too late—' she whispered.

'It's never too late as long as there's *this* between us,' he said, and pulled her into his arms.

Part of her had known this was inevitable from the

moment he'd arrived, yet she was still taken by surprise. If she lived to be a hundred it would still be a shock to feel his lips crushing hers and his arms like steel about her. Once he'd kissed her with tenderness, and the dawning of some feeling to which she hadn't dared to give a name. But now there was only the drive to enforce his own will. No tenderness, just the sheer blind power of a man who understood nothing else.

He wrenched off her robe, tossing it to the ground, and there was only gossamer silk between her nakedness and Steven's plundering hands. The nightdress might not have been there for all the protection it offered. Through it she could feel every light caress, every intimate touch. He was treating her without respect or courtesy, forcing her to acknowledge the desire that made a mockery of all other feelings. But her pounding heart told her that he was paying her the tribute of a fierce passion that was out of his control.

He was kissing her quickly, tracing a line along her jaw with his lips, then down her neck to her throat. 'It was always going to come to this,' he murmured. 'We took too long to face it—far too long—'

'David—' she whispered frantically.

'Forget him. This is what matters now. No woman has ever affected me the way you do.'

One of the straps of her nightdress snapped under the urgent movements of his fingers. He was kissing her neck, her shoulders, her breasts. Jennifer fought not to respond, but the feelings he could evoke in her were stronger than will. They could make her forget sensible resolutions and think only of him and how he could force her to want him. She was so totally absorbed in him that she wasn't even aware that he'd drawn her towards the bedroom, and through the door…

'Jennifer…'

She looked up into Steven's face, but he hadn't spoken. He'd become still and pale at the sound of the voice that had come from her bed. She felt him grow tense with shock. Slowly he drew away from her, his eyes fixed on the bed. David was just sitting up, a hand covering his eyes.

For a long moment the world froze. At last David dropped his hand, stared at them for a moment, then fell back again with his eyes closed.

'You deceitful little jade,' Steven said slowly. 'You did it again.' He was white with anger as he pulled her out of the bedroom.

Jennifer tried to clear her head. Her body was still singing from his touch, and she could hardly grasp the calamitous nature of what had happened. She flinched at the savage look in Steven's eyes.

'Steven, you don't understand—'

'What is there to understand? You knew how I felt about you and you let me make a fool of myself showing you. And all the time—you were laughing at me. *Again!*'

'I wasn't,' she cried wildly. 'It's not the way you think—'

'You'll be telling me next I didn't see David Conner in your bed,' he raged.

Her own temper rose to meet his.

'And so what if you did? He happens to be my fiancé. What man has a better right to be in my bed?'

'At one time I could have given you an answer to that. But that was before I realised you were stupid enough to take this farce seriously.'

'I'll do as I like,' she cried. 'How dare you come here dictating whom I may and may not marry? You were so sure of yourself. Snap your fingers and Jennifer would come running, because she couldn't possibly love another man if Steven Leary wanted her.

'But you were so wrong. Everything I've ever done has been for David. He's the man I love and nobody else could mean anything to me.'

'You've been playing with me…' Steven whispered.

'Yes, I've been playing, but so have you. You've got no complaint, Steven. You just found someone else who could play the game better. How does it feel?'

'Like being knifed through the heart,' he said quietly.

His answer shook her to the depths. For a moment his face was wiped clean of all except raw pain. She had a blinding flash of awareness, such as a fencer might feel when, after duelling for a few rounds, she discovered that the buttons had fallen from the foils. Suddenly it wasn't a game any more. The buttons were off, the blades were sharp, and the pain was terribly real.

She had one brief glimpse of anguish in his eyes. If it had lasted longer she might have reached out to him, but the shutters came down at once, leaving only bitter vengeance behind.

'There's an old saying, Jennifer,' he said in a voice of deadly quiet. '"Fool me once, shame on you; fool me twice, shame on me." I actually let you fool me twice, and I can't leave it there. Nobody treats me the way you have. Nobody deceives me, then casts me aside. I win every game.'

'You haven't won this one,' she flung at him.

'The game's not over yet. It won't be over until I've won and you acknowledge it.'

'You'll wait a long time for that.'

'If I have to wait for ever, my moment will come,' he said bitingly. 'But it won't take that long. You'll wish you'd never made an enemy of me. Remember I said that.'

He took a step towards her, and it was all she could do not to back away. There'd always been an underlying hint of menace about Steven, but now it was more than a hint. It was there, it was real, and it was turned against her.

'Get out of here,' she breathed.

'When I'm ready. I've something to say first. Go ahead and marry your pretty boy. You'll regret it in a week. And when he drives you crazy, with his weakness and petulance, remember how it could have been between us. You and I could have made the stars envious. And you threw it all away.'

Then he was gone, leaving her staring at the door, trembling with shock.

Jennifer was awoken by a light kiss on her forehead, and opened her eyes to find David beside her.

'I've brought you a cup of tea,' he said.

'Oh—thank you. How are you this morning?'

'Fine. Those headaches never last long, thank goodness.'

He was looking better, smiling contentedly. Which was odd, she thought, for someone who'd seen his fiancée kissing another man the night before. But perhaps he hadn't seen it. For much of the time his hand had been over his eyes. And sometimes, she knew, his mind blocked out the worst of his headaches.

She sipped the tea, and found it delicious. David had many domestic talents.

'You were right about the champagne,' he said. 'Luckily for me you were there.'

She wished he hadn't said that. Once she'd loved to

hear how he relied on her, but now it seemed to lay fetters on her. She'd got him into this situation, and she couldn't turn away from his need.

Then it came back to her, the thing she'd been trying to remember, on the beach when Steven had said, 'I'm glad you were with me when I found out.'

Need. The eager hold on a comforting hand. She'd associated those things with David, but they'd been there too in Steven. This was the elusive echo that had troubled her, and she'd remembered when it was too late.

She and David had breakfast together like an old married couple. Then she dropped him at work and went on to her own office, where Trevor was waiting for her. He spoke some conventional words about her engagement, but his eyes were troubled.

'You are happy, aren't you?' he asked at last.

'Deliriously,' Jennifer declared.

'It's just that Maud thought things were happening between you and Leary.'

'I was stringing him along for the firm,' Jennifer said. 'That's over now.'

'Your break-up with him has lowered our price, but only a little,' Trevor said. 'It'll climb again.'

But to everyone's dismay the price went into a steep drop that seemed to grow faster with every hour. 'Someone's unloading our shares,' Trevor said, aghast.

In despair Jennifer realised that Nortons was on a downward slide to oblivion. But suddenly the price halted, and began to inch back up.

'The rumour is that one man is buying us up,' Trevor said. 'And he probably owns enough now to demand a seat on the board. To make matters worse, Barney wants a board meeting this evening—and he's going to be there.'

Barney arrived ten minutes before the meeting was due to start, and surveyed the boardroom with its neatly arranged chairs about the oak table. 'We need an extra chair for our newest board member.'

'But we don't know who he is,' Trevor said patiently. 'And he isn't going to turn up because he doesn't know there's a meeting.'

'Anyone smart enough to pull this move is smart enough to arrive at a meeting nobody's told him about,' Barney declared firmly.

At precisely five minutes to six the three partners were ready. Barney took his seat in the high-backed chair at the head of the table.

'Mr Chairman, would you like to begin?' Trevor asked formally.

Barney shook his head. 'Let's wait just a little longer.'

Jennifer and Trevor glanced at the empty chair, almost expecting to see it inhabited by a ghostly presence, so strong was the force of Barney's conviction.

At that moment the large grandfather clock in the corner began to strike six. All of them sat transfixed as the sonorous sounds filled the room.

As the vibrations from the last note trembled into silence the door opened, and Steven Leary entered the boardroom.

CHAPTER TEN

IN THE moment of total silence Trevor jumped to his feet. Jennifer rose slowly. Only Barney stayed where he was, apparently unperturbed.

'Good evening,' Steven said. 'I hope I haven't kept you all waiting.' He spoke to them all, but his eyes were on Jennifer and they were made of stone.

'You mean it's you who's been buying us up?' Trevor demanded.

'Not him,' Jennifer said. 'Charteris.'

'No,' Steven said coolly. 'Me, personally. I now own a third of Nortons.'

You'll wish you'd never made an enemy of me. His words echoed in her head with terrible significance. Steven Leary had come for his revenge.

'I think we should welcome our new board member,' Barney said, smiling. 'The best way forward for us all is to try to get along.'

'I agree,' Trevor said.

'Don't either of you understand what's happening here?' Jennifer demanded wildly. 'You have to fight him or he'll swallow us whole.' She turned on Steven. 'Barney doesn't understand about you, and Trevor doesn't want to fall out with Maud's brother, but I see through you and I'll fight you.'

'You've made your position very clear,' Steven said. 'Now I wonder if we could get to business.'

He took his place at the table, leaving Jennifer stand-

ing there, aghast. It was clear the other two didn't see
the danger.

But she'd known Steven as they hadn't. She'd felt the
power of his arms about her, seen his face above hers,
heavy with passion, then dark with rage. Once she'd
seen it gentle, vulnerable, when he'd told her simply that
he trusted her totally. Now trust had turned to bitterness.

Steven distributed some papers, pushing Jennifer's towards her without a glance. She studied them and felt a
chill at the efficiency and thoroughness she found there.
Glancing up, she found him looking at her. He'd followed her thoughts, and wanted her to understand that
it was just as she'd feared.

Calmly he laid out his plans. He planned for the firm
to do a lot of business with Charteris, which meant that
Nortons would have to expand, at great cost.

'Once we've gone in this deep, Charteris will have us
in its pocket,' Jennifer protested. 'They can force down
our prices, then drive us under and buy us up cheap.'

'I suppose you'll just have to try to trust me,' Steven
said coolly.

'Jennifer, my dear, it's not like you to be prejudiced,'
Barney protested.

Even Trevor was making noises of approval as his
eyes swept the pages. Jennifer knew she'd lost this
round.

'There is one thing,' Trevor said as Steven prepared
to depart. 'How did you know about this meeting?'

Steven gave a smile as cold and bleak as winter.
'When a man is determined to do something, then he'll
usually manage to do it. And believe me, I'm very determined.'

His words were general, but his eyes were on Jennifer.
The next moment he was gone.

                    *   *   *

A week later Steven's work was interrupted by a commotion in his outer office. He threw open his door, and, as he'd expected, he found a furious Jennifer.

'Come in,' he said distantly. 'I can give you five minutes.'

She hadn't seen him since the board meeting. He seemed thinner, and there were dark shadows under his eyes.

'It won't take me that long to tell you what I think of you,' Jennifer said. 'Of all the unscrupulous, devious— I've just been talking with Barney. How dare you tell him that I should postpone my wedding!'

'You can't start your honeymoon just as Trevor is returning from his.'

'I thought I knew how low you could stoop—'

'You were wrong,' he interrupted her coolly. 'You haven't begun to discover how low I can stoop. You may find out yet.'

'I'm not postponing my wedding at your command.'

'Then I'll just have to take a more active role in Nortons while you're gone.'

Jennifer froze as she saw the trap into which he'd lured her. 'You'll take a more active role over my dead body.'

'But you won't be there,' he pointed out.

'You devil,' she breathed. 'And to think that I—'

'*That you what?*'

She was struck dumb. There was suddenly nothing to say.

His secretary looked in. 'Your next appointment is here. Shall I ask him to wait?'

'No need,' Steven said. 'Ms Norton is just leaving.'

It was as though he'd switched her off. Jennifer

paused in the doorway for a last horrified look at him, but he'd turned away.

'I've postponed the wedding for a month,' she told Maud with a sigh. They lunched together regularly these days. 'I had no choice.'

'I don't know what you did to make him so bitter,' Maud said, 'but it really got to him. Mind you, after he tried to scare David off in that heavy-handed fashion I wouldn't blame you for anything. It's strange of Steven to be so clumsy. Usually his judgement and timing are spot-on. He must be in love with you after all.'

To Jennifer's dismay this suggestion caused a flutter of agitation deep within her. To hide it she said, 'What a dreadful prospect!'

'Oh, heavens! Not you as well!' Maud said plaintively. 'Between the two of you I'm getting squashed. What happened to make my brother go out of his mind?'

Jennifer told her everything, right up to the moment Steven had discovered David in her bed. 'He thinks I made a fool of him, and to him that's unforgivable. He won't stop until we're just a subsection of Charteris.'

'Actually, Charteris is a bit cross with Steven for not getting them better terms from Nortons. They think he takes Nortons' side too often.'

'How do you know?' Jennifer asked.

'Because he tells me everything. Naturally he swears me to secrecy.'

'And you promise?' Jennifer asked.

'Of course. Otherwise he wouldn't tell me, and then how could I tell you?' Maud asked logically. 'You mustn't let on to him that you know.'

'No chance of that, since we're not on speaking terms. I don't understand. What scheme is he working on now?'

Maud considered a moment, before saying, 'I'd better tell you something else. How do you think Steven got the money to buy thirty per cent of Nortons?'

'I've always wondered about that.'

'The bank made him a huge loan, but he had to put up his Charteris shares as collateral.'

'He did *what*?'

'He's in the same boat as you, Jennifer. If anything happens to Nortons he loses everything.'

Jennifer was stunned. Whatever Steven was doing, he was committed to it in deadly earnest. But he wasn't acting from love. She inspired his passion, but these days it was a cold, vengeful passion that left her apprehensive.

'Try to understand him,' Maud begged. 'Steven's been fighting most of his life, for Mum, for me, and only lastly for himself. He doesn't know anything else. He's forgotten how to say please.'

'It's nice of you to try,' Jennifer said wanly. 'But it really doesn't make any difference now.'

She drove home slowly, feeling as though life was closing in on her like a prison. Secretly she was glad of the excuse to delay her wedding. She would have escaped if she could, but the memory of David saying, 'You take such good care of me,' was with her always. She'd fought so hard to win him, and now his need seemed to shackle her.

Despite their quarrel she missed Steven desperately. It wasn't merely desire that united them. There was a tough, astringent quality to his mind that appealed to her. They could laugh together, and read each other's thoughts, because they complemented each other. She could have loved him, if only he'd loved her. But he'd gone out of his way to tell her that he wasn't in love with her and wouldn't make a commitment to her. It was his pride he was avenging, not his heart.

That last bitter scene in his office had been like a door slamming. The hurt was bad, but it would have been even worse if she'd been in love with him. It was some consolation that at least she was safe from that. She must cling onto the thought. Because otherwise life would be unendurable.

There was some justice in Maud's complaint that she was caught between the two of them. Mostly her brother stayed at work late these days, but that evening she found him at home in a black mood.

'For heaven's sake, do something,' she told him. 'Reach out to her, before it's too late.'

'It's already too late,' he growled.

'I lunched with Jennifer today and she told me what really happened the night you called at her flat.'

'What is there to tell? She was in bed with her fiancé.'

'But she wasn't. He had a migraine from drinking champagne and she took him home and put him to bed. She slept in the spare room.'

He gave a crack of ribald laughter. 'My God! Would you listen to that?'

'If Jennifer says it, I'm sure it's true.'

'True?' he roared. 'Of course it's true. It's just the kind of witless performance I'd expect from that ninny.'

'Well, I suppose the poor man can't help the way he's made.'

Steven got up and strode to the door, as though movement eased his tension.

'I'll tell you this,' he said contemptuously. 'If I was naked and lying in the bed of the sexiest woman I've ever known, I'd sure as hell think of something more inspiring to do than *have a headache.*'

The phone call that turned Jennifer's world upside down came in the middle of one afternoon.

A young man said, 'I'm Constable Beckworth. We have a man in the cells at Ainsley police station. He was arrested for brawling and he asked us to call you. His name is Fred Wesley and he says he's your father.'

Jennifer took a long, slow breath to counter the feeling of being punched in the stomach.

'Ms Norton?'

'I'll be right there.'

She was functioning on automatic as she drove to the station. Her father had arrived back in her life after sixteen years, and she couldn't think straight.

He was older, thinner, his hair grey and straggly. He looked like a man who'd lived rough for a long time. But he had the same perky grin that had won her heart as a child.

'The bad penny turned up again,' he said. 'Pleased to see me?'

'Let's get you out of here,' she said, avoiding the question.

They didn't talk on the journey, although he whistled at her shiny car. With his shabby clothes he looked incongruous against the soft leather.

He whistled again when he saw her home. But all he said was, 'Nice.'

'I'll get you a meal,' Jennifer said.

After so many years missing him, longing for him, wondering why he never made contact, now she felt all at sea. She didn't know what to say. He was a stranger—until he gave his cheeky grin again, and that made her smile. But at the same moment came a slight chill. She wondered how much he relied on that grin, and instinct told her that it was too much.

'How did you know how to contact me?' she asked as she moved about the kitchen. Fred stood watching her, a glass of wine in his hand.

'Saw a piece about the old man in a magazine,' he said. 'It mentioned "Trevor and Jennifer Norton".'

'He changed our names when we were children,' she said quickly. 'We had no say—'

'Don't worry. The old's boy's rolling in it, you get your hands on some.'

'That's not—' she began to say, but he'd already turned away and was studying her living room.

'Very nice,' he said, drawing the words out. 'Done well for yourself.'

'Why did you call me and not Trevor?' she asked as they sat down to eat.

'Don't think he'd have given me the time of day. We didn't get on well when he was a kid. But you and I were always close.'

'So close that you walked out on me and never got in touch,' she couldn't help saying.

'I was only thinking of you. Barney never liked me. I reckoned if I wasn't there your mum could go back to him and he'd see you all right.'

'So it was an act of generosity for our sakes?' she asked quietly.

'That's right. A father's love.' There was the grin again.

'Dad, don't,' she said tensely. 'I'm glad to see you again, but you don't have to feed me all that stuff.'

'Well, whatever. You did all right for yourself, and that's the main thing.'

'What happened to that woman you went to live with?'

'Oh, her! We broke up. Easy come, easy go.'

'Like buses,' Jennifer said quietly.

He roared with laughter. 'Hey, that's not bad. A bit like buses, yes. I tried my hand at this and that, but the luck was against me.'

'You might have stayed in touch.'

'Barney told me not to,' he said, just too casually. He saw her disbelieving eyes on him and shrugged. 'Well, you were better off without me. Look at this place. Very nice. Very nice indeed.'

Jennifer ground her nails into her palm, wishing he'd stop saying 'very nice'. She'd imagined this meeting for years, but now it was here and he was a man she didn't know and was finding hard to like.

She struggled with the feeling. His image had lived in her heart too long for her to dismiss it easily now. Somehow their reunion must be made to accord with her dreams.

Things would be better next day. A good night's sleep would change them both for the better. She made up the bed in her spare room, ensuring that he had every comfort.

He seemed glad of an early night. As she'd suspected, he'd been sleeping rough, and he'd drunk two bottles of wine with very little help from her. When he was snoring she called Trevor. Her brother exclaimed, but didn't react as caustically as he would once have done.

He arrived early next morning and the three of them had breakfast together, but Jennifer could see that Fred had been wise in not calling Trevor. Father and son had nothing to say to each other. Trevor was painfully stiff and polite. He mentioned his coming marriage, and after a few conventional words Fred asked, 'Pick a girl with a bit of money, did you?'

It was a measure of Maud's softening influence that this question offended Trevor. He visibly winced, and changed the subject. As he was leaving he said to Jennifer in a low voice, 'I didn't like him years ago and I don't like him now.' He touched her arm gently. 'If you've got any sense you'll keep him at arm's length. Don't let him hurt you.'

'He can't hurt me after all this time.'

'I hope not. I'm afraid you're about to get sentimental about him.'

'Well, he is our father. I'm going to spend today with him.'

She had been beginning to fear the worst, but the day turned into an unexpected pleasure. Fred was on his best behaviour, making her laugh and squiring her to lunch with great charm. It was true that she picked up the bill, but it was still enjoyable to be sitting there with him. Somewhere deep inside her a tense knot of muscle began to relax. It wasn't too late. The past could be repaired.

She kitted him out with some new clothes, including a couple of suits, and had to admit that he looked splendid in them. They dined at the Ritz that night, and she began planning how they would spend the next day.

'Why don't you go to work in the morning,' he suggested, 'while I go and see your mother's grave? We'll meet up for lunch.'

Next morning she told him how to find the churchyard, and arranged to meet him at the Ritz at twelve-thirty. She left early for lunch and stopped off to buy him a silk tie.

She reached the restaurant ten minutes early, and ordered an aperitif for herself and him. She pictured his face when he arrived and found everything ready for him.

Twelve-thirty and no sign of him. He'd probably forgotten the time. She wondered which of his new suits he would be wearing.

Twelve forty-five. Perhaps her watch was fast. She checked with the waiter and found that it was actually twelve-fifty.

She ordered a mineral water and sipped it slowly, trying not to listen to the ominous murmur of fear in her heart. Of course he was coming. He would be here by one o'clock.

At one-fifteen she stopped pretending to read the menu. Perhaps something had happened to him. She ought to call home. She dialled on her mobile but there was no answer. Perhaps he'd got lost.

Perhaps he wasn't coming.

She dialled again. It might have been a wrong number. But again there was no reply.

Perhaps he wasn't coming.

She began to say it to herself. He's not coming. He's not coming. It throbbed through her head so persistently that she imagined she heard a voice saying the words. Then she realised that the voice was real.

'He isn't coming,' Steven repeated.

She looked up as he sat down opposite here.

'How do you come to be here?' she whispered.

'We share a family grapevine now. I know all about it. Did you really think he wouldn't let you down again?'

'It's—not the same.'

'Yes, it is, Jennifer. It's exactly the same. He's a man who runs out. He ran out on you then and he's run out on you now. I expect he's done pretty well out of you. How much did you spend on him?'

It was the truth, and she'd never run away from the truth.

'A lot,' she said. 'All right. So now you know. Will you please go away?'

'Not until I've said a few things.'

How could he torment her now? she wondered. However much he hated her, how could he do this?

'Please go away,' she said tiredly.

'This was always a mistake, Jennifer. He can't reach back into your childhood and make it right, and nor can you. What he did he did, and it helped to make you the person you are, a woman who needs safety and reassurance from a man—or thinks she needs it.

'But it doesn't have to be like that. You're stronger than you know. Strong enough to say good riddance to him.'

'You know nothing about it.'

'I know that you can put all that behind you if you really want to. Don't let this destroy you. You're strong enough not to.'

'I don't feel very strong right now,' she admitted. The tense knot was starting in her stomach again. 'I just want to—'

'Give up? Don't say that. Don't even think it. Stand up on your own. You can, you know. You don't need anyone as badly as you think you do. Not your father, not David, not me. Keep telling yourself that, because it's true. And maybe you'll still be in time to avoid the disaster you're walking into. That's all.'

He got up and walked away without another word, leaving Jennifer staring after him almost in shock. His words might have been meant as a sort of comfort, but he'd uttered them without once softening the harshness of his face and voice. He'd handed her the key to surviving this experience, but he'd done it without warmth. He was as hostile as ever but he'd given her the strength to overcome her pain. Or rather, he'd pointed out her own strength.

There was no sign of Fred when she went home. All his new possessions were gone, plus he'd taken her best suitcase to carry them. Her new chequebook had been removed from her desk. In its place was a note, saying simply, *Sorry, love, but you don't begrudge me, do you? Fred.*

For a dreadful moment she was swept back years. She was alone, with no points of reference in a hostile world, and a chill wind was whistling about her. She flinched back into herself, seeking refuge from that wind, longing for a place where she could crawl away and hide.

But Steven's voice pursued her. 'You're stronger than you know…stand up on your own.'

It was true. Steven had seen the truth about her more clearly than anyone else. And he'd come seeking her out to offer his fierce, uncompromising comfort, knowing that it would be her truest support.

She saw David that evening, and related almost the whole experience. But she didn't mention Steven.

'My poor darling,' he said, taking her hand. 'What a terrible thing to happen to you.'

'I don't know,' she said thoughtfully. 'In an odd way it was useful. It laid a ghost. Perhaps I'm better off without that ghost.'

'I can imagine what it must have done to you— brought back the past, traumatised you.'

'But does bringing back the past have to be traumatic? Maybe it happens so that we can deal with it and make it really the past? It's strange. I never thought of that before. But I should have.'

'Darling, you're so wonderfully brave about it,' David said tenderly. 'I wish I'd been there to help you.'

'I had help,' she murmured.

'I know I haven't been much use to you recently. I feel I've failed you. But not any more. From now on I'm going to be everything you've always wanted me to be.' He gathered both her hands in his. 'I'm here for you, Jennifer, and I always will be. Once we're married I'll never leave you. We'll be together all our lives. That's a promise.'

CHAPTER ELEVEN

MAUD was happy to exchange her glamorous life for domesticity, but she wanted to go out in a blaze of glory. Her wedding dress had to be expanded just an inch.

Jennifer went with her for the final fitting, and was full of admiration. The traditional gown was long and romantic, with a train and a veil streaming behind her.

Jennifer had been uneasy with Maud's request that she be bridesmaid, but Trevor had been eager for her to agree, and she had reluctantly done so. If Steven was to be her brother-in-law, she couldn't spend her life avoiding him.

Maud had chosen Jennifer's dress herself, with an unerring eye. The result was silk of the palest peach, cut and draped in a style that was sophisticated, elegant and faintly Grecian.

The reception was to be held in the huge garden at the back of Steven's house. When Jennifer arrived there early on the morning of the wedding the marquee was up and caterers were already scurrying back and forth.

There was no sign of Steven, and Maud confided that he'd gone out earlier, saying he would return later. Jennifer wondered if he was avoiding her.

Maud's favourite hairdresser arrived and set her hair in huge rollers. Then she put him to work on Jennifer, giving so many detailed instructions that he asked which one was the bride.

'I am, but I'm fine,' Maud said. 'I want Jennifer to look just right.'

She applied her own make-up with swift, professional movements, then worked on the bridesmaid's face herself. An uneasy suspicion was gathering in Jennifer.

'You're wasting your time making me look good,' she said. 'I'm marrying David, and even if I weren't, your brother is the last person I'd choose.'

'Funny, he says the same about you,' Maud said, putting the last touches to Jennifer's left eyebrow. 'Only more forcefully.'

When her hair was finished Jennifer had to admit that Maud knew what she was doing. Delicate, wispy curls floated about her face, giving it a flattering softness. The peach threw a warm glow on her skin, and her dark eyes seemed larger than usual, thanks to Maud's artful magic.

'I'm just dying for a cup of tea,' Maud said prosaically.

'I'll go down and get you one,' Jennifer offered.

It gave her the chance to practise walking in the delicate silver sandals that went with the dress. By the time she'd made it to the bottom of the stairs she was moving easily. She sighed with relief and looked up to find Steven standing there, his gaze fixed on her.

She'd been concentrating so hard that she hadn't seen him enter. Now she caught him off guard, and the look in his eyes, before he controlled it, showed her everything he would have preferred to keep hidden. She saw his shock at her transformation, and one moment of naked longing, before he brought down the shutters.

After a moment he spoke, through lips that seemed stiff. 'I didn't know you'd arrived.'

'Maud and I have just finished getting ready. I'm fetching her a cup of tea.'

'No time. The cars are here.'

'I'll tell her.'

Just a few banal words, but they left her feeling as if she'd been through a wringer. She wondered how she was going to endure today.

At last it was time to depart. Maud swirled down the staircase in a cloud of glory to where Steven was waiting for her in the hall below. Jennifer helped her into the car, carefully arranging the gorgeous dress so that it wouldn't crumple. Steven opened the front door and prepared to get in.

'You're supposed to sit with me,' Maud protested.

'It's better if your bridesmaid is with you,' he said in an expressionless voice, seating himself beside the driver.

On the short journey to the church Jennifer refused to look at his back. She was remembering what Mike Harker had told her. *Steven said weddings were a female conspiracy for making men look ridiculous, and he'd never let it happen to him.*

Today was the kind of occasion he'd meant, to be endured only for Maud's sake. No doubt he thought of herself as part of the conspiracy. He'd made it plain often enough that all he'd wanted from her was an affair.

When they reached the church Steven waited while Jennifer adjusted final details of the bride's appearance. At last he offered Maud his arm, and they began the procession to the church.

They were a few minutes late, and when the organ struck up Trevor looked around and smiled at his bride, in joy and relief. She smiled back, and their mutual happiness lit up the church. She had full and complete possession of Trevor's heart, Jennifer reflected, and she needed nothing else.

She remembered the night Paws had given birth, and

Steven joking about her sounding 'like a medieval tyrant saying, "Bring me the head of Steven Leary."'

But it was his heart she wanted. And nobody could bring her that because he didn't have one.

And yet he'd sought her out when her father had deserted her for the second time, offering her something that hadn't sounded like sympathy but which had done her more good than David's conventional comfort. Rough as Steven's words had been, they'd steadied her as surely as—she sought for the comparison and found the one that had been waiting all the time—as a hand held out in the darkness.

She bowed her head over her bouquet, suddenly swept by a tide of misery. She would never admit, even to herself, that she loved Steven. But the pain would go on and on, and she didn't know how she was going to bear it.

Inwardly she cried out at Steven for his heavy-handed attempt to part her from David. But for that she wouldn't have known the moment of rashness that had made her insist on the engagement. Now she was trapped, bound to David by his need of her—a need which, in honour, she could never betray—and by his conviction that she needed him.

Maud took her place beside her groom, and the service began. Steven gave his sister away, then stood back. He never once looked in Jennifer's direction, but she knew he was conscious of her, as she was of him.

At last the organ pealed out triumphantly. The bride and groom swept from the church, and the congregation followed.

At the reception Jennifer was joined by David, who kissed her cheek and told her she was beautiful. They sat together during the speeches, receiving several smiling glances from people who obviously knew that they were next.

Afterwards Trevor and Maud led the dancing on the lawn, shining with love and happiness. Jennifer danced with David, conscious that Steven, having avoided her until now, was watching her with burning eyes. She wondered if he would ask her to dance, or rather, demand a dance, since that was more his style.

But instead he took the floor with one of Maud's model friends, a young woman so stunningly beautiful that Jennifer couldn't bear to watch. She slipped away, hoping nobody would see her, and wandered across the lawn, into the trees.

But even here there was no peace, because it reminded her of the enchanted night when she'd wandered with Steven in Barney's garden. She'd laughed with him, and teased him in a way that now seemed the height of madness. Why had she never suspected the dangerous path she was walking? Because she'd been falling in love, and that was the most dangerous thing of all.

On the far side of the trees she came to a patch of land where workmen were busily clearing bushes and levelling the ground. Metal spikes had been driven into the earth, with light ropes slung between them, apparently outlining the shape of buildings.

'What's this?' she asked curiously.

One of the workmen stopped and gave her a friendly grin. 'Not sure, really. We've been told to clear the ground.'

'But these outlines?'

'They've been moved a dozen times, and I guess they'll move a dozen more. He keeps changing his mind.'

'But what's it going to be when it's finished?'

'Well, as far as I know—'

'What are you doing here?'

Jennifer turned to see Steven behind her, frowning.

'I was curious,' she said. 'You don't mind my looking at your garden, do you?'

'I don't like your being here,' he said curtly. 'It's not safe in those fancy sandals. The ground is uneven.'

He took her arm, steering her firmly away. She could sense his anger, and knew that concern for her safety was only a cover. This was a secret, something else from which she was shut out.

'Did you see your father again?' he asked as they walked back across the lawn.

'No. When I reached home he'd gone, taking my chequebook—which he made good use of.'

'Good,' he said coolly. 'You're better off now. But I dare say you don't think so.'

'Yes, I do. I'm grateful to you, Steven. You really helped me. I wonder why, when you hate me.'

'I don't hate you. Despite everything I respect and admire you. I thought it would help you see sense about Conner.'

'I'm still going to marry him. He needs me and he's good to me. If you could have seen him when I told him about my father—'

'I'll bet he offered you a life of tender protectiveness and cotton wool. You'll suffocate in a month.'

'I gave him my word.'

'Break it, Jennifer. Break every promise you ever made rather than go through with this and destroy us both.'

She gave a wan smile. 'I don't think you're that easily destroyed.'

'I want you. I've never made any secret of it—'

'Yes, and I know why. Another man's woman. A challenge to your possessiveness. But it's not enough. Just think of me as a bus, Steven. Passing by, and out of your life.'

'Out of my life? With my sister married to your brother? We'll never be out of each other's lives. In a few months we'll have a mutual nephew or niece.'

'Then I'll wave to you at the christening. And so will my husband. I'll be married to David by then.'

'The devil you will!'

'I will, because my word is my bond. That was the first thing Barney ever taught me. He said it went for life as well as commerce.'

He gave a bark of cynical laughter. 'I can just hear the biggest twister in the business saying that. How many times did *he* wriggle out of awkward commitments?'

'Nobody knows,' Jennifer admitted. 'But he always managed to look like the soul of honour while he was doing it. Steven, please try to understand. How can I desert David *now*, when I've just been reminded how cruel it feels?'

'Don't ask me to understand, because I can't. I'm not soft-hearted like you. I take what I want, when I can. I'll never go through this kind of fancy performance, but I could give you a life worth living.' His face was dark with suffering. 'I should say I wish you happiness for the future, but I can't tell such a lie. I wish you the same future as mine—a life of bitter regret and wondering what might have been. Goodbye, Jennifer.'

When the bride and groom had departed for their Caribbean honeymoon, and the guests were drifting away, Barney found Steven alone in the garden, deep in a very large whisky.

'I'm ashamed of you,' he declared.

'I'm not driving,' Steven said, surprised. 'This is where I live.'

'I'm not talking about the drink. I'm talking about you, giving in without a fight. And you have the nerve to say I was your mentor. You never learned that from me.'

'I've tried fighting,' Steven growled. 'But it doesn't get me anywhere. In fact, it was fighting that created this mess, according to Maud.'

'Wise woman. But you still aren't a credit to my example. And after all I've done to help you.'

'I know that. I'm grateful to you for warning me of that meeting.'

'But I did it for a reason, lad. I want Jennifer out of this engagement as much as you do, and I believed you were the man to do it. But you've fumbled it badly.'

'All right, what would you do?'

'Well, first, I wouldn't have got myself into this situation, but that's because I know Jennifer so well.'

'Of course, she's your granddaughter. If she was *my* granddaughter *I* wouldn't have got into this situation,' Steven complained.

'The way you're going, you'll never have a granddaughter,' Barney riposted. 'Not with Jennifer.'

'Well, that suits me fine. Because if you think I'd marry that pig-headed, obstinate—'

'Are you in love with her or not?'

'Yes, dammit!'

'Then we have to take firm, decisive action. All we need is David Conner's weak spot.'

'Oh, I can tell you that,' Steven observed.

He did so. The old foxy gleam came into Barney's eyes. 'That's it!' he crowed. 'One last scam, just as I promised myself. Here's what we do.'

When he'd finished talking Steven poured himself another drink. 'It won't work,' he said. 'Even David Conner would never be that much of an idiot.'

'There's no end to the idiocies a man will commit when he's in love,' Barney declared. 'After all, look at you.'

Steven scowled.

CHAPTER TWELVE

'WILL you take this woman to be your lawful wedded wife…to love and cherish her—?'

Steven gave her a smile full of love as he said, 'I will.'

But then his face turned into David's, and Jennifer cried out that this was the wrong man. She would have run from the church but David clung to her.

She awoke to find herself sitting up in bed, shaking, with tears pouring down her face.

'Oh, God,' she wept, 'not again.'

She sat there in the darkness for several moments before she could find the strength to get out of bed. She was becoming desperate to avoid these dreams, but they pursued her every night.

She went into the kitchen to make herself some tea. As she worked she brushed away the tears, but more flowed in their place. At last she sat down, staring into her cup, and let the tears come as they would. It was better to weep now, when nobody could see her.

It wasn't always the same dream. Sometimes she began by marrying David, and he changed into Steven, who smiled and said, 'You didn't think I was going to let you marry another man, did you?'

That one was the hardest because it touched a nerve. Secretly she'd always expected him to stop the wedding. She knew that Maud had passed on the facts about the night he'd found David in her bed, and that he'd believed them, so surely they no longer had any quarrel? But he'd done nothing.

She wasn't sure what she'd expected, but she couldn't imagine him sitting tamely by while he lost the woman he wanted. Burn down the building, kidnap the groom, the bride, the whole wedding party. Steven was capable of all that before accepting defeat.

But he didn't want her; at least, not enough to make a commitment. That was the truth she had to face. At the very moment when she'd finally understood the depth of her love for him, he had shrugged and lost interest. For him, there would always be another bus along soon.

Now here she was, the night before her wedding, breaking her heart over the man who'd scorched across her life and vanished, leaving her desolate.

She hadn't seen or spoken to Steven for weeks. He'd sent a wedding gift of antique silver, accompanied by a formal note wishing her every happiness, and she'd written him an equally formal letter of thanks. After that there had been only silence.

She'd seen little of David, too, as he'd been away in Scotland, hunting suitable sites for Nortons depots. Barney had entrusted him with this mission as a way of welcoming him into the family.

Barney's reaction to her engagement had been strangely muted. He liked David, but he hadn't been eager for the marriage. She realised that he'd fallen under Steven's spell.

Even her brother was getting on well with Steven, whose hostility had faded in the face of Trevor's devotion to Maud. Trevor too would have been glad to see her marry Steven, but he'd welcomed David politely, and, by telephone from the Caribbean, had offered him the use of his new four-wheel drive car for the trip over rough terrain.

The whole Scottish idea had puzzled her. David's brief had been to investigate the islands, but to Jennifer these were the wrong places to site new depots. She had an uneasy feeling that Barney had created the job out of courtesy, apparently forgetting that David had a firm of his own to run.

He'd returned much later than expected, and with only vague explanations. At last, reluctantly, he'd told her the true reason.

'When I was on the isle of Arran, Trevor's car was stolen. The police expected to find it easily, because the last ferry had gone, and there was no way of getting it off the island until the next day, when they could mount a watch. But it seemed to have vanished into thin air. I kept holding on, hoping it would be found, so that I wouldn't have to return without it.'

'But you drove it home,' she said. 'So you got it back.'

'After a week it simply turned up in the hotel car park. It wasn't damaged. Nothing had been taken from it. Even the petrol tank was full.'

'But that's weird. What do the police think?'

'They're as baffled as I am. It had been wiped clean of fingerprints, so there were no leads. You don't know what a relief it was to be able to start for home and stop having to make unconvincing excuses for the delay. Luckily your grandfather didn't seem to notice anything odd.'

'Barney usually notices things,' Jennifer said, puzzled.

'Maybe he's being tactful. I've given him my report but when I ask him about it he just puts me off. I'm not sure he's even bothered to read it. He probably thinks I'm a complete no-hoper.'

'Of course he doesn't,' Jennifer said warmly. She felt

the old protective tenderness for this gentle man. But mingled with it was a twinge of dismay that he needed to be bolstered all the time. She couldn't help thinking of how differently Steven would have reacted, cursing up hill and down dale, never caring who knew his car had been stolen as long as he got it back fast. In fact, it was hard to picture anyone daring to steal Steven's car.

David had seemed very quiet that evening, but she'd put that down to tiredness and strain, for the trip had plainly taken a lot out of him. He'd excused himself from seeing her very much before the wedding, arguing that he had to work long hours at his business to get everything in shape before he left for their honeymoon. Jennifer had acquiesced with a feeling that she'd guiltily recognised as relief.

Since then they'd barely met or spoken, and she'd been left with a sensation of being in limbo, caught between the two men, but in touch with neither of them.

And in a few hours the day would be here when she must commit herself to a man she was fond of, but whom she did not love. David was charming and kindly, but he lacked the steel that her ideal man must possess. Not that the steeliest man she knew was in any way ideal. He was arrogant, overbearing, impatient, rude and unforgettable.

She didn't return to bed, not daring to risk another dream. Besides, it was already growing light. Maud would soon be here to help prepare the 'happy bride'. She pulled herself together, and by the time Maud arrived the tears had been washed away and Jennifer could manage a smile.

Maud was lightly tanned from her honeymoon. Her waistline was increasing rapidly now, and, as she happily confided, she was longing to wear her first maternity frock.

The bridal outfit was a short cocktail dress in cream silk, topped off by a small matching hat. Maud made up Jennifer's face expertly and stood back to admire her handiwork.

'You look lovely,' she said. She glanced out of the window. 'Barney's car has just arrived. Shall we go?'

'Just—just a moment,' Jennifer said. 'I'm not quite ready.' She needed a little more time, to ignore the pain in her heart, and force herself to go ahead with this.

But at last there was no delaying it any longer. She gave Maud's hand a squeeze, and went out to where Barney was waiting for her.

The three of them said little on the way to the register office. Jennifer covered her pain with a fixed smile, and the other two seemed strangely uneasy. Barney filled the awkward silence by chattering about his coming great grandchild.

'Are you sure you're taking care of yourself?' he asked Maud for the hundredth time. 'You still look as though a breath would blow you away.'

'Don't you worry about me,' Maud told him. 'I'm a lot stronger than I look.'

You're stronger than you know.

Jennifer sat up straight with shock. Maud's words had opened a door in her brain, and through it walked Steven, as he'd been when her father deserted her again.

'You're stronger than you know…stand up on your own…you don't need anyone as badly as you think you do. Not your father, not David, not me.'

It had taken until now, when it was almost too late, for her to see what was staring her in the face. Steven had wanted to detach her from David for his own unscrupulous reasons. Blinded by that, she'd overlooked the simple truth. Steven had always understood her better than anyone.

She couldn't marry David. She was too fond of him to do him such an injury. She must break off this marriage now, and then she must tell Barney she was withdrawing from the firm. If he demanded back the shares he'd once given her, she would return them with a light heart, and somehow she would make him understand that it was time she reclaimed her own life.

What that life would be, it was too soon to say. But she knew abandoned animals would come into it somewhere.

And Steven? She simply had no idea what would happen between them, but she would confront him as a free woman: free and strong, as he'd shown her how to be.

All this flashed through her mind with the speed of light, less conscious thoughts than a series of blinding images. The decision was taken before the others could ask her why she was staring into space.

'Barney, have you got your mobile?' she asked breathlessly.

'Of course not,' he spluttered. 'Not on my way to a wedding.'

'Stop the car!' Jennifer cried.

She bounded out and ran frantically to the nearest telephone box. She must try to catch David before he left home. But the phone was answered by his mother, just about to depart.

'David went out an hour ago,' she said. 'He said he'd catch up with me there.'

Jennifer dived back into the car. 'I can't tell you anything yet,' she told the others breathlessly. 'It's just—I just—can't tell you.'

It was David's right to hear it first. But if only it didn't have to be at the register office! She failed to see the quick glance between Barney and Maud, or the way they both crossed their fingers.

Jennifer's heart was beating hard when they arrived. The next half-hour was going to be difficult, but she wouldn't weaken. If only poor David wasn't too badly hurt.

Some of his family were there already, and soon his mother arrived, looking anxious. 'I thought he'd be coming in the car with me,' she explained. 'But suddenly he said he had something important to do first. Oh, dear, I do hope he gets here soon.'

There was a small commotion, and heads turned. But it was Steven who entered. His face was harsh and set, and for a moment Jennifer thought he would come to her. But then he turned away, and she knew that he wouldn't try to stop her marriage. And that refusal would colour all their future relationship. If any.

Then her head went up. Steven himself had said she was strong enough to do without him, and she would prove it true, no matter how much her heart ached.

The time of the wedding came and went. The next party was ushered in first. Jennifer looked around, baffled. Normally David was as punctual as clockwork. It was part of his soundness, the quality that he used instead of inspiration.

Suddenly there was a hum in the little crowd. Turning, Jennifer saw David standing in the doorway, but not as she'd expected him. He wasn't dressed for a wedding, and he wasn't alone. Penny was beside him, holding his hand.

Pale and tense, the bride and groom faced each other

in the middle of the room. Jennifer took a deep breath, but David spoke first.

'I'm sorry, Jennifer,' he said. 'I can't marry you. I'm in love with Penny.'

The words seemed to hang in the air. Jennifer stared at him, too astounded to take in the look of triumph that flashed between Steven and Barney.

'Jennifer,' David pleaded. 'Please say something.'

The town hall had witnessed jilted brides before, but never one who let out a shriek of delight and hugged her ex-groom with relief.

'I'm so glad,' she wept. 'Oh, David, I'm so glad.'

'You—you are?'

'I wasn't going to go through with it either,' she confessed. 'We should never have got engaged. It was all my fault. Try to forgive me.'

'You're the most splendid woman in the world,' he said in relief. 'Too splendid for me. I think I've been falling in love with Penny since the night of the gala, but at first I wasn't sure. Then we were stranded on the island together—'

'Penny was there with you?'

'Your grandfather forgot to give me some important files, so she had to follow me up there. The night she arrived the car was stolen, and she was a tower of strength—'

'Of course,' Steven murmured.

'And our feelings were just too strong for us. I—' He looked at Penny, who squeezed his hand encouragingly. 'We felt the best thing was to be open about it.'

'How wise!' Steven said sardonically. 'And there's nothing like leaving it to the last minute.'

'Will you hush?' Jennifer said, digging him in the ribs. She was full of relief, but her joy was tinged with disappointment. Steven hadn't tried to halt her marriage. In one sense, little had changed.

David turned away to explain to his mother, who was looking bewildered. Jennifer thought she would soon be glad of the change. She knew that the little woman was slightly alarmed by herself. Penny would suit her far better.

Trevor and Maud were hugging each other with glee, and Jennifer was baffled to see Steven and Barney shaking hands vigorously, and laughing.

'The fox hasn't lost his touch after all,' Barney declared triumphantly. 'I did it.'

'*We* did it,' Steven said, his eye on Jennifer. 'I'm going to need my share of the credit for this. Although I'll admit you were the brains.'

'What are you two talking about?' Jennifer demanded.

'I'm surprised you need to ask,' Steven said. 'Did you really think I wasn't going to sabotage this wedding?'

'But what did you do?' Jennifer begged, her heart leaping.

'We gave David the chance to discover that he really loved Penny,' Steven said.

Barney joined in. 'I sent him to Scotland on a wild-goose chase. And then I sent Penny after him. I wanted him to take her in the first place, but he wouldn't—'

'He was being noble on your account,' Steven said wryly.

'Something you wouldn't know anything about,' Jennifer said, indignant at his tone.

'Not a thing. You won't catch me being noble where my own interests are concerned.'

'Never mind that,' Barney said, quelling the squabble. 'I invented the story about the files, so she had to follow him.'

'But the stolen car—?' Jennifer said, bewildered.

'That was the easiest of all,' Steven said. 'The "thief" worked for me, and he was armed with Trevor's spare key, with Trevor's permission. So he simply drove it away without trouble. He took it the night Penny arrived, locked it up in a private garage, and left it there for a week. Then we just had to sit back and wait while your fiancé's feelings overcame his scruples.'

'Something else you wouldn't understand,' Jennifer said.

'I've never had any scruples about taking what I wanted,' he agreed. 'But you almost defeated me with your crazy obstinacy.'

'Me? If you think—'

'Be quiet, woman, and kiss me,' he said, firmly taking her into his arms.

Her heart sang with the kiss from the man she loved, a kiss she'd thought she would never know again.

'That's it!' David cried suddenly. 'Now I remember.'

Everyone turned to look at him.

'The night we got engaged, I saw you two together when I woke up, but I was half-blind from the headache and it didn't properly register. Next morning I knew I'd seen something important, but I couldn't remember what. It's been driving me crazy, and now it's come back to me.'

'It's a pity you didn't remember sooner,' Steven growled. 'You might have saved us all a lot of trouble. Now, push off, there's a good fellow, and get yourself engaged again.'

'Actually, I already have,' David said, with a proud look at Penny.

'Fine.' Steven confronted Jennifer. 'That just leaves

us. I have something to say to you, and listen well, for I may never manage to say it again.

'I nearly lost you because I didn't know how to tell you how much I love and need you. I can't imagine the rest of my life without you. But, thank God, that isn't going to happen. We found each other in time.'

It was the declaration of love she'd longed for, and her heart seemed to take wing and soar with joy. Yet even now his self-assurance was just a little too much. If they were to be happy she needed to stand her ground at the start.

'An affair, I think you said,' she challenged him.

'Never in a million years,' he said emphatically, 'will I have an affair with you. We are getting married. Otherwise you might try to marry some other man, and I couldn't stand the strain of all this again.'

'An affair is what you wanted,' Jennifer said, equally emphatically. 'And an affair is what I'm offering.'

'Excuse me,' the registrar interrupted them, 'but is the Norton-Conner wedding going ahead or not?'

'Not,' Steven said firmly.

'In that case, may I ask you all to leave?'

'Come on,' Barney said. 'We've got all that food laid out at home. We'll have a party.'

'But without us,' Steven said, looking at Jennifer. 'We're going to have a party of our own.' He took her hand. 'Come with me.'

He was striding from the room even as he spoke, cheered on by the others. By Jennifer stopped him in the doorway, just long enough to toss her bouquet to Penny.

'Invite us to your wedding,' she cried, laughing, just before Steven whisked her out of the door.

Before she knew it she was seated in his car, and he was out on the road, driving with fierce concentration.

'You've spent too long dithering,' he said. 'I told you the first time we met that you were disorganised, and, boy, was it true! From now on I'm taking charge.'

'Of me? Of my life?'

'Of our entire relationship. Never, never again will I let you put me through what you did today.'

When they reached his house he hurried her upstairs, keeping a firm grip on her hand, as if afraid she would vanish if he let go. When he'd shut his bedroom door behind them she demanded, 'Can I speak now?'

'Not while you're wearing *his* wedding dress.' He was fumbling at the tiny pearl buttons down the front.

'Careful, you'll tear it.'

'So what? You're never going to wear it again.' He gave a wrench and the buttons spilled all over the floor. Another wrench and the dress was in pieces. 'That's better.'

'What do you think you're doing?'

'What I've been wanting to do for weeks,' he said, tossing her slip away. The next moment he'd torn off his jacket and shirt, and pulled her hard against his bare chest. His hands fumbled in her hair, tumbling it down about her shoulders, then his mouth was on hers, hot, fierce and urgent.

'I've lain awake dreaming about this,' he said between kisses. 'Night after night—going mad—afraid I'd never have you in my arms again—and you didn't care! You were so cool and composed, and all the time I was in hell!'

His lips silenced her before she could answer, but she responded without words, opening her mouth for his deeply exploring tongue. They clung together, united as much by relief as by passion. They'd been to the edge of the abyss and looked over into a life without each other. And they'd backed off from that life, in dread. The deep, mutual love they'd discovered infused every action with beauty.

Jennifer had often wondered how their first loving would feel. Now she knew she needn't have worried. What was happening now was truly lovemaking, as she'd hardly dared to dream it could be.

Steven held and caressed her as though she were a treasure he'd thought lost for ever. Once Jennifer even thought she saw anxiety in his eyes, but she enfolded him in her arms, laying her lips reassuringly on his, and love cast out fear.

When at last they became one he made love to her with every part of his body, with his loins, his hands, his eyes that watched her with a possessive, brooding passion.

'Is everything all right, my love?' he whispered.

'Everything,' she whispered back. 'Everything.'

Her words—or perhaps something he heard in her tone—seemed to be what he was waiting for. He claimed her more deeply, but with a tenderness that was heart-stopping. She gave it back a thousandfold, and knew that finally all was well between them.

Afterwards they didn't fall apart, but clung together even more closely. Then Steven, the least poetical of men, surprised her with a gesture of pure poetry. Taking her hand, he lifted it high, intertwining his fingers among hers and bending his own so that she was held fast.

'Two becomes one,' he said. 'Do you see?'

'Yes, I see,' she said in wonder.

It was the safety she'd dreamed of but thought Steven could never give her. If she'd known then what she knew now she would have realised that safety lay in the arms of a man who loved you passionately and feared nothing so much as to lose you. The rest was talk.

They dozed for a while, and when they awoke he kissed her. 'Did I hear you tell Conner you wouldn't have gone through with it either, or did I imagine that?'

'No, I really said it. I made up my mind in the car. You were right. I'm stronger than I knew. I'm leaving Nortons too. I have to find out where my life is heading.'

'It's heading down the aisle, with me.'

'I said I wouldn't marry you. Weren't you listening?'

'I never listen to nonsense. I love you. How about in six weeks' time?'

'And I love you, too. But have you any idea how outrageously you've behaved? Moving people around like pawns, sending David and Penny here and there, getting them stranded just to suit yourself—'

'And aren't you just glad I did? Them too.'

'That's beside the point.'

As she spoke she was letting her fingers drift down his chest, across his flat stomach, and lower, to where she could already see the growing urgency of his need.

'If you imagine,' she purred, 'that I'm marrying a man whose idea of polite conversation is to give orders—'

'Orders? Me? I'm the soul of meekness.' Steven drew a shuddering breath, trying to control himself against what she was doing to him. He had something to say, and it was important to get it out before she drove him completely crazy, but Jennifer spoke first.

'Who told me—"I'll never go through this kind of fancy performance"?'

'Never mind what I said then,' he growled. 'Listen to what I'm saying now.'

'Who also told me that I was strong enough to stand

alone, because I didn't need anyone, including Steven Leary?'

'I was a fool. Jennifer, you're winding me up—aren't you?'

'Partly,' she mused. 'I know I can stand on my own two feet now, and you did that for me.'

'Now get this into your head once and for all,' he said raggedly. 'We are getting married. Not in a register office, but in a church. You're going to wear white satin, carry flowers and look glorious. I shall wear a morning suit and look sheepish and ridiculous, as befits a groom. But it doesn't matter because nobody will be looking at me. They'll be thinking how beautiful you are, and how lucky I am.

'Trevor will be my best man, and he'll wear the smug expression of a man who's already been through it and is enjoying watching the other fellow suffer. It will be a completely wonderful wedding. And afterwards—'

'Afterwards?' Jennifer asked, her heart beating at a sudden new note in Steven's voice.

'Afterwards, I shall never, ever let you go again.' His voice was husky. 'So now that's settled—'

'Is it settled?' she asked mischievously.

'Yes, it is—and do you know what you're doing to me?'

She smiled, an ancient, mysterious smile. 'I know *exactly* what I'm doing to you.'

'It's very dangerous unless you mean it.'

'But I do mean it,' she said joyfully. 'I mean it with all my heart.'

He abandoned the last of his control and took her firmly into his arms. 'In that case…'

It was late evening before they got up, and the sun was low in the sky.

'I'm hungry,' Jennifer murmured.

'Then I'll make you a feast. But first I want to take you outside and show you something.'

'But I haven't got any clothes or shoes here,' she protested, laughing.

He wrapped her in a huge bathrobe of his own, and carried her out into the grounds. The sunset drenched the land in a soft glow, and she snuggled against him blissfully, wondering where they were going, but content simply to be in his arms.

He carried her through the trees, to the place she'd seen on Maud's wedding day. The ground was completely cleared now, and more buildings had been outlined, but work seemed to have stopped.

'It couldn't go any further without you,' Steven explained, seating himself on a huge log, with her on his lap. 'I need your ideas before I start building.'

'My ideas about what?'

'Oh, didn't I mention that? It's going to be an animal sanctuary.'

'A what? *Steven!*'

'It's your wedding present. And in my usual arrogant, overbearing way, I started setting it up before you'd agreed to marry me.'

'A sanctuary,' she breathed in wonder.

'Well, I thought you'd like one. The thing is, I shall still need you at Nortons, at least for a while. But gradually you'll spend less time with the firm, and concentrate on running this place. Even when you give up your job you'll have the income from your shares, and you can use that to pay for the staff you'll need here. I thought one person to start with, but later—'

'Hey, hold on,' she protested. 'You've got it all

worked out, haven't you? What happened to giving me a say?'

'Did I get it wrong? All right, tell me how *you'd* like to manage things.'

'Well—actually—I'd like to do exactly what you've just described. And, Steven, if there's one thing about you that annoys me more than anything else it's the way you can read my mind, and anticipate what I want before I even want it. And cut that out.' For Steven had shouted with laughter.

'Sorry,' he said at last. 'My disgraceful habit of being right all the time is something you'll have to come to terms with.'

Jennifer kicked him with her bare foot, but not very hard.

'So what else am I going to want to do?' she asked. 'Tell me now, and save me the bother of thinking it out for myself.'

'Well, something tells me that you're going to expand the sanctuary until we have to move out to make room for the inmates—'

'Residents.'

'Residents. And don't worry about where they're coming from. There's a local animal charity that's got more waifs and strays than they know what to do with, and they're very anxious to meet you. When you've approved the plans I'll have the men start on the foundations, and then—'

His words were cut off by her mouth, clasped eagerly to his. He was the first person who had ever sympathised with this side of her life, and without words she tried to tell him of her passionate gratitude that he'd understood her needs and wanted to fulfil them.

'So this was the big secret you steered me away from at the wedding,' she said, when she could speak.

'I was going to enjoy surprising you, and you nearly spoiled everything by discovering this place. And by the way, I said it was your wedding present—'

'I'll marry you; I'll marry you,' she said at once.

He grinned. 'I thought this would do it. But actually, I have another present for you. He's just over there, coming to investigate us.'

Jennifer gave a cry of delight at the sight of a small black cat with white paws, bounding across the grass. He leapt into her lap and began nuzzling her.

'Is it really him?' she asked.

'The very same. I sought out that family and told them I wanted Paws Two as soon as he was old enough to leave.'

'But we were going to call him Steven.'

'Don't you dare call him after me,' Steven said severely. 'He's a total idiot. Since he moved in the place has been a shambles.'

She gave a sigh of contentment, and snuggled against him. 'Oh, everything's perfect. To think you started mapping this place out while you hated me.'

'I never hated you. I didn't like you pumping me for information for David, but when you said it was just a practical joke, I guess I always believed you. But my pride had got tangled up by then, and I couldn't think straight.

'It hurt, and that warned me that I was in deeper than I'd thought. So I did everything wrong. I tried to wrest you from Conner by force, instead of coming to you and saying I loved you, which is what I should have done. When my clumsiness had propelled you into that engagement I was nearly off my head.

'I started preparing this place for you as a way of reassuring myself that things would be all right. And all the time I blundered on, making things worse, and your wedding day got closer. I think I went a bit crazy. Luckily, Barney came to the rescue, and we thought up this scheme to throw Conner and Penny together.'

'But, darling, suppose David hadn't jilted me? Did you have a plan for that too? Or would you have just stood there and tamely watched me marry another man?'

Steven gave her his wickedest smile. He put Paws Two firmly on the ground and drew her very close, murmuring, 'My love—my dearest love—what do *you* think?'

MILLS & BOON®

Makes any time special

Enjoy a romantic novel from
Mills & Boon®

Presents... *Enchanted*™ *Temptation*®

Historical Romance™ *Medical Romance*™

MILLS & BOON®

Next Month's Romance Titles

♡

Each month you can choose from a wide variety of romance novels from Mills & Boon®. Below are the new titles to look out for next month from the Presents...™ and Enchanted™ series.

Presents...™

A RELUCTANT MISTRESS	Robyn Donald
THE MARRIAGE RESOLUTION	Penny Jordan
THE FINAL SEDUCTION	Sharon Kendrick
THE REVENGE AFFAIR	Susan Napier
THE HIRED HUSBAND	Kate Walker
THE MILLIONAIRE AFFAIR	Sophie Weston
THE BABY VERDICT	Cathy Williams
THE IMPATIENT GROOM	Sara Wood

Enchanted™

THE DADDY DILEMMA	Kate Denton
AND MOTHER MAKES THREE	Liz Fielding
TO CLAIM A WIFE	Susan Fox
THE BABY WISH	Myrna Mackenzie
MARRYING A MILLIONAIRE	Laura Martin
THE HUSBAND CAMPAIGN	Barbara McMahon
TEMPTING A TYCOON	Leigh Michaels
MAIL-ORDER MARRIAGE	Margaret Way

On sale from 1st October 1999

H1 9909

MILLS & BOON®

MEDICAL ROMANCE™

PRACTICALLY PERFECT by Caroline Anderson

Surgeon Connie Wright found locum G.P. Patrick Durrant deeply attractive and his small son Edward soon found a place in her heart. But Patrick would be moving on and Connie would be returning to London...

TAKE TWO BABIES... by Josie Metcalfe

Maddie's ex-husband had kidnapped her daughter and she was distraught. When Dr William Ward was so supportive, Maddie knew this man was for her...

TENDER LIAISON by Joanna Neil

Dr Daniel Maitland doesn't believe Dr Emma Barnes will stay in his practice—nor does he believe Emma when she says he has a lot of love to give!

A HUGS-AND-KISSES FAMILY by Meredith Webber
Bundles of Joy

Dr Angus McLeod had never stopped loving Jen, his only thought to woo and win her all over again. Discovering Jen was pregnant was *such* a shock!

Available from 1st October 1999

MILLS & BOON®

Makes any time special™

By Request

Bestselling themed romances brought back to you by popular demand

Each month By Request brings you three full-length novels in one beautiful volume featuring the best of the best.

So if you missed a favourite Romance the first time around, here is your chance to relive the magic from some of our most popular authors.

**Look out for
Wedlocked in September 1999
featuring Day Leclaire,
Margaret Way and Anne McAllister**

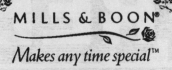

MILLS & BOON®

Makes any time special™

By Request™

Bestselling themed romances brought back to you by popular demand

Each month By Request brings you three full-length novels in one beautiful volume featuring the best of the best.

So if you missed a favourite Romance the first time around, here is your chance to relive the magic from some of our most popular authors.

Look out for
***After Hours* in October 1999 featuring Jessica Steele, Catherine George and Helen Brooks**

Available at most branches of WH Smith, Tesco, Asda, Martins, Borders, Easons, Volume One/James Thin and most good paperback bookshops

FREE

4 BOOKS
AND A SURPRISE GIFT!

We would like to take this opportunity to thank you for reading this Mills & Boon® book by offering you the chance to take FOUR more specially selected titles from the Enchanted™ series absolutely FREE! We're also making this offer to introduce you to the benefits of the Reader Service™ —

★ FREE home delivery
★ FREE gifts and competitions
★ FREE monthly Newsletter
★ Exclusive Reader Service discounts
★ Books available before they're in the shops

Accepting these FREE books and gift places you under no obligation to buy; you may cancel at any time, even after receiving your free shipment. Simply complete your details below and return the entire page to the address below. *You don't even need a stamp!*

YES! Please send me 4 free Enchanted books and a surprise gift. I understand that unless you hear from me, I will receive 6 superb new titles every month for just £2.40 each, postage and packing free. I am under no obligation to purchase any books and may cancel my subscription at any time. The free books and gift will be mine to keep in any case.

N9EC

Ms/Mrs/Miss/Mr ....Initials ....
BLOCK CAPITALS PLEASE

Surname ....

Address ....

....

....Postcode ....

Send this whole page to:
UK: FREEPOST CN81, Croydon, CR9 3WZ
EIRE: PO Box 4546, Kilcock, County Kildare (stamp required)

THE Regency COLLECTION

Where rogues find romance

Look out for the sixth volume in this limited
collection of Regency Romances from
Mills & Boon® in October.

Featuring:

Hidden Flame
by Elizabeth Bailey

and

Ravensdene's Bride
by Julia Byrne

Still only £4.99

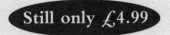

MILLS & BOON®

Makes any time special™